SHADOW OF THE DAHLIA

JACK BLUDIS

PageTurner Editions
A Renaissance E Books publication
San Francisco CA
2010

This book is for Jay, Trev, Max, Kathryn and Linda
With special thanks to Jan Long and Jeremiah Healy for pre-publication
suggestions

CHAPTER I

I started out by looking for a missing blonde and ended up finding justice in an unusual place.

"You're lucky, Rick. I'm the only homicide detective in L.A. who's not working the Black Dahlia case," Sgt. Marco Sandiri said from behind his wooden desk. "Who lost this blonde?"

"Tyree Prendergast," I said.

"The airplane guy?"

"He was. Now he's just crawling with money and he's got a missing wife."

Sandiri had been too old to go to war and too honest to move higher than sergeant even after twenty years as an LAPD detective.

"One of these days, I won't have time to look up this crap for you."

"You don't look that busy."

"I'm on everything *but* the Dahlia, and I'm doing it alone."

"Why aren't you on that one?"

"Why don't you find another cop to irritate? But just to get rid of you, I'll put you in touch with her best girlfriend."

"Girlfriend?"

"They roomed together when they were under contract to MGM. The blonde married rich like you say. The brunette learned how to type and take shorthand. I'm not sure where she's working."

Sandiri fingered thorough the cards in a small, rectangular box. We were friends before the war when I was a rookie detective. He stayed in L.A. while I went into the army. I washed out of flight school and went into airborne infantry. He made police sergeant and I made captain, but Airborne captain didn't convert to anything civilian. It helped me get a private detective's license though.

He read off an address on Doheny Drive in West Hollywood.

"No phone number?"

"She works mostly daytime."

"Typing and shorthand, huh?"

"That's what I hear. You know a snitch named Little Georgie?"

"Red hair, big ears?"

"Talk to him if you can find him – when's dinner?"

"How about tomorrow night?"

That was the deal. We gave each other information, but I always paid for dinner. As far as I knew, it was the closest to graft that Sandiri ever came.

* * * *

I figured if this Dixie Joy had a day job, I'd be wasting my time to look for her now, so I cruised Hollywood Boulevard from Vine to La Brea in my '39 Ford.

The war had been over for more than a year and women were starting to wear cinched waists to show off figures they didn't have. Some men wore open throated sports shirts for leisure, but the business look in L.A. called for ties, jackets and hats. In spite of what the pulp magazines and the paperback novels would have you believe, a private eye is a businessman and not a crusader.

On the third pass on Hollywood, I saw Little Georgie trying to swindle a couple of out-of-towners. After he did business, he hurried away and crossed the street in front of me.

"Hey, Georgie!"

For a second, he thought I was a cop and started to run. Then he did a double take. He recognized my Ford and came back to the passenger-side window. A half-block away, the suckers were already trying the money wheel he had just sold them.

"Get in," I said.

He had to get away fast before they tried to print a second dollar bill. He climbed into the car.

"Let's get the hell out of here," he said.

"How's business?"

"I need a new gimmick."

"Yeah, me too," I said.

Georgie wore the tie and jacket but not the fedora that was standard uniform for guys like me. Besides, the hat would have messed up his ton of red hair.

"What d'ya need?" he asked.

"Sandiri says you might know something about a Laura Prendergast."

"She used to be a hooker." Sandiri hadn't given me that.

"Tell me about her."

He looked over his shoulder to see if the out-of-towners had caught on yet. I didn't see them in the rearview mirror anymore, but we were already two blocks away.

"MGM dumped her with a load of starlets in the middle of the war. She and this girl named Dixie Joy went to work for Sal Trugante."

2

Salvatore Trugante ran red-light houses all the way up to Beverly Hills. He had them all over L.A. County and down into San Diego.

"Guy name of Cameron took on both gals for calls only."

"Cameron took them over from Trugante? You know this to be a fact?"

Georgie snorted. "They got an arrangement. Cameron gets the best girls for calls and he gives 'em back to Trugante when they're over the hill or he can't sell them to private parties. Prendergast bought her from Cameron and put a ring on her. That was about a year ago. What else you need?"

"How about the other one?"

"She's a secretary, workin' for Trugante."

"Trugante? In one of his houses?"

"That's iffy. I'm not sure how she's workin'. She's working out the place where he lives in Laurel Canyon. Daytime kind of thing."

"You got addresses or phone numbers?"

"Nothin' like that. How much am I gettin' for this?"

"So far you haven't told me any more than Sandiri did."

"Did he tell you about the hooker part?"

"Implied. She either walked away from Prendergast or somebody snatched her. What are you hearing?"

I turned south on La Brea and came back east on Sunset. We were passing Hollywood High when he started to talk again.

"Let's get to the brass taxes – how much am I gettin' for this?"

I didn't respond.

"OK, I'll tell you what you need. Cameron's looking for fresh blood. He's givin' back some of the old ones to Trugante."

"Like Laura Prendergast?"

"If she's still a knockout, he'll use her himself."

"Even after he's sold her?"

"Cameron don't scare. If she don't want to stay, it ain't no skin off his ass. Besides, Trugante backs him up."

Most guys wouldn't admit that their wives were ex-hookers, which was why Prendergast didn't tell me.

"You know for a fact that Cameron sold her?"

"That's my interpretation."

"You got an address and number for Cameron?"

"He's in the book, first name Michael. Lives in the Tower on Sunset. Works his girls out of nice places, but not there. He charges lots of big green bills."

"Who's he paying off?"

"Higher than vice," Georgie said.

"Chief?"

He gave me no answer.

"What if I go through all this and I don't find her?"

"Then the next one's on me."

I slipped him five.

"That's it?"

"What do you get for your money wheel?"

"Twenty."

"You have to have them shipped in, you have to find your sucker, and you have to work a pitch. I walked up and bit you in the ass. When I need more information, you get more chances."

"Yeah, like you're gonna make it a point to look for me."

"I did this time."

"Yeah. Okay, I'll take what I can get. Let me out."

I was stuck in traffic just short of Vine Street.

Georgie was out, crossing the street, and combing his fingers back over his big ears making sure that his hair met in the back of his head. He didn't use a comb, but the effect was the same. His hair looked like a duck's ass bouncing on his shoulders.

Georgie's information strung with Sandiri's, but it didn't make a lot of sense. If a woman marries money, why does she go back to being a hooker? In California, divorce was the best path out of a marriage. There was a lot more money in it – a hell of a lot more.

CHAPTER II

It was two o'clock in the afternoon, and if Cameron was handling his business right, chances were good that he would be just getting out of bed. I drove out to the Tower on Sunset and asked the guy on the desk to put me through to his room. He made a connection through the switchboard and handed me the phone across the marble desk.

"Mister Cameron?"

"What are you up to, Paul?"

I wasn't Paul, but I decided to go with it. "I'm looking for a big blonde you had a couple of years ago. Laura something."

"Who is this?"

"Paul."

"Bullshit. Get out of the lobby or I'll have somebody throw you out."

"You wouldn't do that."

"Watch and listen," he said and he hung up.

In about six seconds the switchboard buzzed and the guy on the desk picked it up. "Yes," he said, "Yes, of course."

He looked past me to the big, dumb-looking guy who sat trying to read Sunday's funnies.

"Thank you," I said and I walked casually out the front to Sunset Boulevard and waited on the wide steps.

"Who you think you are?" the big guy asked me.

He was probably the house dick. He wasn't much taller than I was, but he was wider. He had a broken nose and cuffed ears. Now that he was up close, I recognized him as Mickey Wren, a pug who once stayed three rounds with Joe Louis.

"Hey, Mickey! Long time no see. You still fighting?"

He squinted.

"'39. Detroit. If the Bomber hadn't sucker punched you, you'd be wearing the belt now."

"You saw that?"

"I never been to Detroit, but I heard about it. I saw you stay with Two-Ton Tony though."

"Sumbitch wouldn't go down."

"He should've. You beat the hell out of him. How've you been anyhow?"

"Eh, doing a little body guardin'."

"For Cameron?"

"'Leventh floor, yeah. Guy's got more broads than Gable."

"He bring 'em to the hotel?"

"The Tower? Not a chance. Big stars in there. Lots of class."

"You know him from the old days?"

"Before he lost all his cash, you mean?"

"Yeah," I said, but I wouldn't know Cameron from Harry Truman.

"He used to be rich back east. He's doing somethin' with girls now."

"Not pimpin'?" I tried to sound incredulous.

"Hey, I don't talk about people on the backside. But he sure knows how to get 'em."

"Ever seen him with this one?" I slipped the folded glamour photo out of my pocket and showed it.

"What d'ya want her for?"

"Don't want her. Just want to know if she's been around."

He frowned as if something had suddenly dawned on him. "Where do I know you from?"

"I used to hang around the gym."

"You don't look like no pug."

"I just skipped rope and punched the bag. You gonna fight again?"

"Doc says I got too much jelly up here." He touched the side of his hat brim. "Nah, I wouldn't do that again. It could kill me."

"Tell Cameron I was asking about him," I said and I walked around the building to the parking lot.

"Who should I say was askin'?"

"We go way back," I said. Then I stopped and waited for him. "What about the girl?"

"Oh, yeah, Saturday night. Some party down at the Roosevelt."

"What happened to her?"

"Left with some guy. Little guy. Walked straight as a needle. Looked like a fairy. Round hat like Charlie Chaplin only gray."

"Where'd they go?"

"Cab took 'em someplace. I knew the driver."

"What's his name."

"I call him 'Seven-Twenty-Nine' because it's his cab number. Wilshire Cab. Where I know you from again?"

"The gym."

"I ever fight you?"

"I never fought. Just hit the bag. Thanks." I walked toward my car and he shouted after me again.

"What's your name so I can tell the boss?"

I kept walking, but he didn't come after me. I got in my car and drove over to the Wilshire lot. I asked who was driving taxi number seven twenty-nine late night Saturday and early Sunday morning.

"He's coming in now," the squeaky-voiced dispatcher said.

The man who came in was in his late twenties. I told him who I was and what I wanted. He didn't even have to go to a dispatch sheet.

"Took them up to some house on the hill north of Franklin." He looked surprised for a moment. Then he gave me the address on Misty Crest Road. Apparently, he was as good with numbers as Mickey Wren was, but his brain had a whole lot less jelly.

"What did you think about them?" I asked and I gave him one of my business cards.

"Like a hooker and a mark?"

"How old was she, do you think?"

"Twenty-five maybe?"

I showed him the photo.

"Yeah, could be."

"And him?"

"Fifty, maybe sixty. I can't tell with old people."

* * * *

The cab driver was a piece of luck, I thought as I turned left off Highland Avenue and started toward Misty Crest Drive among flat-roofed and terracotta-roofed houses. I went too far on Misty Crest and had to double back. I pulled to the side, looked at the address I had written on the back of one of my cards and at the addresses where I had stopped. If such an address existed, it was in some never-never land between where one set of numbers ended and another began.

So much for luck.

I drove back to the dispatch office and asked for the driver, but he was already on the street.

"Does he have a two-way radio?"

"Wilshire, two-way radios? What do you think this is, Yellow Cab? We're a small outfit."

"Thanks," I said. I gave him my card. "Ask the kid to call. If he gets my service, tell him to leave a number where I can reach him. Or maybe *you* can give me that."

"I ain't the payroll department," the dispatcher said in his squeaky little voice.

"How do you get him when you need him?" I slipped him another dollar.

"He's our best driver. Makes his own hours. He usually brings the cab back by two in the a.m. But Saturdays he works all night. Sometimes on Fridays too, but last Saturday, definitely."

Even with that answer, something didn't seem right.

"Do you have his log?"

"What's this all about?"

"I'm a private detective."

He pocketed the money and went over to a wooden file cabinet to pull out a manila folder. He fingered through the sheets, held one against his chest and put his hand out. Another dollar wasted, I thought, but that was the going rate for a little bit of information.

Someone had printed the log with neat, block letters in pencil. I noted that the driver's name was Paul France.

"Paul, huh?"

"That's him."

I glanced down at his entries near one a.m. The closest I could come was 12:45, a drop off at the Roosevelt. At 1:40, he made a pick up at Cahuenga near Franklin – almost in my back yard. According to the log, he dropped that fare off at the Roosevelt, too. He took nine more fares over the next four hours picking up two of them at the Roosevelt and taking one to the Beverly Hills Hotel, another to the Tower on Sunset.

The time and distance between the Roosevelt drop off and the Cahuenga pickup would allow plenty of time to high flag in the neighborhood of Misty Crest. I planned to come back for an explanation, so I wasn't going to rat out the driver, not yet.

CHAPTER III

Doheny Drive was the street where West Hollywood ended and Beverly Hills began. I waited behind a taxi that had stopped across the street from the address Sandiri gave me. A good-looking brunette climbed out and hurried up to the porch on the West Hollywood side.

I drove around the block and couldn't find a parking space. I didn't think that I would be very long, so I parked behind a new green Pontiac at the Dixie Joy address. I rang the bell three times before the brunette pulled open the door and looked out through the screen. She was wearing a terry cloth bathrobe and towel turban and she smelled of Ivory Soap. I heard music playing on a radio in the background.

"Miss Dixie Joy?"

"Yes? What may I do for you?" Joy was a good name for both of her former jobs, and the way she played up her accent, sultry and Southern, it sounded like she might still be doing one of her old jobs – and it wasn't the movies.

She was tall and trim and the sash on her robe cinched her waist. Everything she had was in just the right places. If she hadn't looked at me so suspiciously through the screen, she might have been beautiful.

"I'm looking for a friend of yours, Laura Prendergast. I think Fane was her movie-star name."

"She was never a star anymore than I was. Her husband sent you I'll bet." She was playing up the "ahs" of her already exaggerated accent.

"Good guess. Do you know where she is?"

"No, I do not. And if I did, why ever would I ever tell you?"

She wasn't the kind of woman who would take a dollar or even five bucks for an answer, but she might take a hundred or more for an hour or two of pleasure. She was probably worth it, but she was way out of my price range.

"Were you with her at the Roosevelt Hotel Saturday night?"

"How ever do you know that?"

"I find out things. Did she run away from her husband?"

"I do not have the vaguest notion. I never spoke to her, but she was doing something quite dangerous."

"Like what?"

"She was leaving the hotel with a strange little man. He did not seem like my idea of a safe date. Are you a police man?" She actually made "policeman" two words.

"Private."

"So I do not have to speak to you at all, do I?" She started to close the door behind the screen.

"Not unless you want to keep your girlfriend safe."

She opened the door wider. "Is that a threat?"

"I think she might be in trouble."

She turned her head and looked at me askance. Then she pushed open the screen-door and gestured for me to step inside. She had kept most of the door between us until now, but she must have known that if I wanted to get in, I could have pushed through with little more than a nudge.

The living room was large, with three overstuffed chairs and a sofa. The house seemed well cared for, but the chairs could have been there since before the depression. There was nothing on either of the two cocktail tables. The only things on the end tables were the lamps.

The floor-model radio against the stairway had just finished jingling out a toothpaste commercial, and Les Brown's Band came on with Doris Day singing *Sentimental Journey.*

Fear gripped me for just a moment, but it was a remembered fear. I was dreaming that song when they woke us and told us that the Germans had broken through at the Ardennes. The song went through my head many times over the next couple of weeks, especially as I tried to sleep when we were surrounded at Bastogne. Until then, the song soothed me. Now, it was the stuff of nightmares.

"Are you okay?" Dixie Joy asked.

"Fine." One of these days or nights I'd stop reacting to the song, but not yet. It was only a little over two years ago.

"Are you certain you are all right? Would you care to sit down?"

She gestured to the sofa and left the room in a hurry. She had a nice, natural swing to her walk and I pushed the Ardennes into my subconscious where it belonged. She brought me a glass of water and I smiled.

"I do not plan on givin' you anything stronger than water."

"Wasn't expecting it."

"What has happened to Laura?" She pronounced it "Low-rah."

"Nothing that I know of. Why did she leave her husband?"

She tasted her own water and looked at me over the rim of her glass. She had nice eyes and she knew how to flirt with them, but she didn't have a lot of confidence that I would fall for it.

"Didn't His Majesty the Millionaire tell you?" she asked.

"She didn't leave a note. Didn't say anything."

"So *he* says."

"So he does. Do you want to tell me what she says?"

"Will you stop lookin' for her if I do?"

"Looking for people is what I get paid to do, and Mister Prendergast is paying me very well."

"It's the same old story, isn't it? She was swept off her feet by this rich fella who promised to love and cherish and all that other boll shit, and what does he do? He orders her around, watches her every move."

"Happens in the best of families."

"But not to Laura. She was lookin' for happiness, not money. And definitely not some man to order her around."

"Is that why she's turning tricks again?"

"She was *not* turnin' tricks. She was just lookin' for a good time." Miss Joy was trying to learn from me while I was learning from her.

"A fairy in a bowler hat? Is that her idea of a good time?"

"She was *not* turnin' tricks! Where are you getting' this information."

"So she was just going with the old fairy for fun?"

"Will you please watch your mouth!"

"Which one of those was the bad word?"

"*Fun.* The way you said it was ugly."

"It was meant to be. Have you seen her since Saturday?"

"No, I have not."

"What was going on at the Roosevelt?"

"A party. Hollywood types, but not Hollywood types – if you get my meanin'. We were entertainin' some investors. People who want to put money into the studios and other people who want to sell their studios. We were *not* doin' tricks."

"You mean not unless Trugante told you to."

"I believe it is time for you to leave." She pointed to the door with her glass as she rose from her easy chair. Some of her water sloshed over her wrist and onto the old, oriental carpet.

"Don't you care what happened to her?"

She gave no answer. I didn't rise from the sofa. I tasted my water and used my eyes over the rim, the way she did. I was trying to intimidate, not to charm – and it worked.

"Do you think you can find her?" She seemed genuinely concerned.

"If you help me. Who was this guy she left with?"

She shook her head and I waited for her to clarify. "I have never seen him before."

"An investor?"

"No, an inventor. He has come up with some kind of film process. Wide screen something or other with lenses. They want to get a jump on television. Something about seein' movies in three die-mensions and the screen goin' from one wall of the theater to the next or somethin'."

"Who were they selling to?"

"I don't know. Laura didn't know them either."

"Did Cameron?"

"It was Mister Trugante's party. Mister Cameron was just caterin'."

"Is that what they call it these days?"

"That is what Mister Trugante calls it. The hotel provided the food and drinks and Mister Cameron provided the entertainment."

"I find it hard to believe that a place like the Roosevelt would allow something like that."

"How long have you been in L.A.?"

"Fifteen years, counting before the war."

"You sound like a tourist. You can buy anythin' in L.A. if you find the right people and are willin' to pay the right price."

She was right. Every once in a while I slipped into a fit of stupidity. In Los Angeles, everything was for sale and anything could be bought – even a wife or a floor of rooms for prostitution in one of Hollywood's best hotels.

"So what was the party about?"

Her eyes shifted across the room to the radio. She stared at it for what was probably no more than a second. Then she looked at me again. Doris Day had long finished singing and they were speaking a commercial on the air. "Paint your car and have it look like new for just twenty-nine dollars."

"I already explained the party," Dixie Joy said. "Inventors and pitch artists, trying to sell gimmicks for movies. And others trying to scare everybody about television."

"Television?"

Television was pictures in a box that I had seen only in bars. With Gable and Crawford still around, I didn't think it would keep anybody out of the theaters, but I didn't know a damn thing about television or movies. All I knew was what I liked.

"Did they sell anything?" I asked.

"I saw the presentations. I am not sure they sold anythin', but they scared the hell out of some of the big shots."

"And the inventor, the one with the bowler hat? You haven't seen him since?"

"Not since Saturday. Not him and not her."

"I know about Cameron and Trugante. Can you give me the names of some of the other people who were there?"

"No." It was the first time she used one word, when she could have used a bullshit answer – or a "boll shit" answer as she would call it.

I raised my eyebrows.

"I have a position, Mister Page. I do not give out information connected with that position."

"I don't have a position, I just have a job. I'd think you would want to help your girl friend."

"Help her to get back to that bastard, Prendergast? Not on your life."

We looked at each other for a long moment. I don't make moral decisions about my jobs unless they go way into the ugly. The jobs I do take, I do as best I can. This job now was to find Laura for her husband and that was what I was going to do.

"What else did she tell you about Prendergast?"

"Will it change your mind?"

"Probably not."

"Then she can tell you – if you find her."

"Why won't I find her?"

"She was talkin' about going home to Cleveland."

People were always talking about going "back east." Hardly any of them ever meant it. Dixie Joy, what a phony name. Her accent was so heavy that I figured it was phony too. She was putting up with a lot of questions. As long as she was answering, I would keep asking.

"Because she was homesick?" I said.

"Because she is afraid of Prendergast." She held her gaze to prove her sincerity.

While we were talking, the six-thirty news came on the radio. The announcer told us that Harry Truman might appoint a former general as Secretary of State and that the LAPD still had no major clues about the killer of the woman that they called "The Black Dahlia."

"If you hear from her, ask her to give me a call," I said.

While she looked at the card I gave her, the next piece of radio news grabbed me: "Just a few minutes ago an as yet unidentified man was found dead behind the wheel of a taxicab not far from our KTL Radio studios. We will have more on that story as it breaks."

My office was just across the street from the Hollywood Palladium and the KTL studios, but what caught my attention was that the dead man was behind the wheel of a taxicab. I did not like to think it, but he was probably Paul France, the cab driver who had given me some misinformation about Laura Prendergast.

"Son of a bitch!"

"Now what is it that you are son-of-a-bitchin' about?" Dixie Joy said, grinning at me.

If the story I just heard on the radio played out the way I was afraid it would, Laura Prendergast was in more trouble than she could imagine.

CHAPTER IV

The sky was fading to dark blue. It would soon be black, but I could still see cops working with artificial light and flashing pictures on the parking lot behind my office building. There was a Wilshire taxi with both doors open. It didn't take a genius to put together the scene here and the KTL story to know that this was where the murder had happened. People were lined up and looking across the lot.

When I started as a private eye, I quickly learned that the police don't like civilian eyes and ears around a crime scene, especially when the civilian has a specific concern. It complicates their job and sometimes puts the civilian in the position as adversary or even suspect. I was involved in too much of that lately, so instead of taking the outside stairs to my office, I called Sandiri from a pay phone.

I told him about the scene and about how I had been asking questions about a cab driver earlier. The call was not so much to keep him informed as to keep him off my back.

"Are you sure it's the same cabbie?"

"No, but what are the odds?"

"Shit! Yeah, what are the odds? Meet you there in fifteen minutes."

I looked across the lot to where three plain-clothes cops were working. More than a dozen people were gathered and talking about the incident. Others just walked by, glanced and went on about their business.

"I hope he's not hurt too bad," someone said.

"Somebody killed him," someone else said.

I was listening closely, hoping to learn something that I didn't know, but thoughts of Dixie Joy kept distracting me.

"Hey, Rick!" It was Sandiri. He reached across the front seat of his personal car and opened the door for me.

"Aren't you going down there?" I said.

"I'll see the reports in the morning. I want to know what you've been up to."

"I thought you said you were the only homicide cop not working–"

"I am, but I'll let the Hollywood detectives do the preliminary. You didn't tell me enough. Get in and give me the details."

I told him about everything, including the gap in the cabbie's log. I gave him the address where he was supposed to have taken Laura Prendergast. We drove up there together, but there was still no house by that number. I gave him the same second-hand description of the guy wearing the bowler.

"You think something happened to her?" I asked.

"If he keeps the hat, we'll have him in nothing flat."

"He's supposed to be an inventor."

"How do you know that?"

"Some kind of convention over the weekend at the Roosevelt."

"Where'd you get that?"

"General information," I said.

"Sounds specific to me."

"I made some contacts," I said, and I gave him the details.

"I'll check it out tomorrow, or I'll have somebody else do it, but I don't think this one's going to be my case."

"Just as long as you don't sic them on me for knowing too much."

"They'll be suspicious, just like I usually am. But since you had nothing to do with it, you should be okay. Right?"

"Yeah."

I was pretty sure I would end up having *something* to do with it. The dispatcher heard me talking to the cab driver. The driver gave me a phony address, one that wasn't on his log. He might have grabbed the address out of the air because he wanted to cover his ass, but he also knew I was looking for something important. Apparently, it was something that somebody wanted to hide pretty deep.

"Can you check his log right up to the murder?" I said.

"I'm sure the Hollywood guys will, but you won't get the information from me, not in an ongoing case. We can still have dinner tomorrow, but we won't talk about this one. I'm going to go down and see what they found out."

I told him some of what I learned, but not where I learned it. He never asked if I found Dixie Joy or Little Georgie.

* * * *

My apartment is in four-storey building just above Franklin – a living room, kitchen, bedroom and bath. What more does a man need? I put my hat on the clothes tree and called the answering service for messages.

"Oh, yeah, Mister Page. Let's see. Calls from Mister Prendergast, a Miss Joy and somebody named Georgie. Georgie didn't leave a number or a last name. He said you would know where to find him."

"Georgie, huh?"

"That's what he said."

I thanked her and leaned back in the chair. Logic said that I should call Prendergast first, but I had been thinking about Dixie Joy since I first saw her, so she got priority.

"Did you find her?" she asked as soon as she heard my voice.

"That quick? Is that why you called?"

"Now why else would I call you?"

"Of course I haven't found her. But you have some more information, don't you?"

"You are goin' to think this is odd, but can you pick me up at the Larabee? Do you know where that is?"

"Near the Goldwyn Studios."

"Pick me up now. Would you please?"

I liked the sound of that. "Give me a couple of minutes."

I should have called Prendergast before I left the apartment, but right now, my brain was doing less thinking than the part of my anatomy that doesn't get nearly enough exercise.

As I turned the corner to go to the lot behind my building, a big guy stepped from the shadows.

"Page?"

"Yeah?"

I didn't hear anyone behind me, but something hard was pressing under my shoulder blade. "The boss wants to talk to you," he said.

He patted me down and took the .38 from my shoulder holster.

"This way, Mister Page."

He directed me to a guy in his fifties who was holding open the back door a limousine. He gestured me inside with a silver-plated automatic and I was sure he knew how to use it. He motioned with the gun again, this time for me to move against the opposite door. He gave off the distinct aroma of cologne. The other guy closed the door. There was nobody in the front seat.

The guy who sat across from me had a bird's-nest toupee and was wearing a million-dollar suit. It always amazed me that men who could afford suits like that would wear such rotten headgear. But who was going to tell him he looked stupid?

"Do you want to tell me what this is about?" I asked.

"It's about you fucking my daughter," the man with the bad rug said. I figured him for "the boss."

"Who's your daughter?"

"Don't you know who I am?"

I thought I might be in trouble for not knowing, but he had never been my boss, at least not that I knew about.

"No, sir. I don't know you. I'm sorry."

Sir almost always goes well when you're talking to someone who's holding a gun, unless he thinks you're being sarcastic and that was definitely not the case here.

"My name is Salvatore Trugante."

What a coincidence, I thought. And now I knew exactly how he fit with the word *boss*, but I didn't remember seeing him before.

"Good to meet you, Mister Trugante." I would have offered my hand, but it would have taken an awkward twist of my body, and he might think I was going for a backup piece.

"Do you know my Alice?"

"I know a couple of Alices."

"Don't be smart. I'm talking about Alice Trugante."

"I don't know anyone by that name. No, sir."

"She give you another name?"

"Sir?" I shook my head.

"You're a polite boy, a smart boy. You should get people's names right."

My mind was bouncing around with Alices. I thought of a brunette before the war and a young blonde right after I came back. Neither looked like she could be the daughter of this guy, but I had to ask. "Alice Smith?"

"That the name she gave you?"

"I'm not sure. Just a guess."

"Blonde. Little. Beautiful."

Good-looking maybe, but not quite beautiful. I had the right Alice though.

"Yes, sir. Alice Smith," I said.

"And where did you meet this Alice Smith?"

About a year ago, she interrupted me reading the newspaper at the Yucca Café and asked me to buy her a drink. I didn't think her father would want to hear that, so I didn't mention it.

"I met her through a friend," I said.

"What friend?"

"Trevor Foxwell. Blonde guy. Tends bar at a place on Cahuenga."

"Now why did you want to pick up a girl as young as that?"

With a guy like Trugante, you had to come up with better than right answers. You had to come up with answers that he would accept. "Trevor said she was a good kid. We talked–"

"And you fucked her?"

"Mister Trugante, a girl like her–"

"What about a girl like her?"

"A nice girl like her, you don't just do what you just said. You talk to her. You have dinner someplace. You–"

"And did you?"

"Have dinner? Yes, sir." Actually, it was breakfast at an all-night diner before we went back to my apartment. We had dinner a couple of nights later and we had sex each time.

He sighed and looked out the door at a taxi that was letting somebody out in front of my apartment house. He kept a firm grip on the automatic. Finally, he looked back at me. "How was she?"

"She was a nice girl. We went out a few times."

"And the last time you saw her?"

"Seven months ago, maybe eight."

"That's what she says too. You're out of the noose. You're a private dick, right?"

I hated the tag "Dick." It fit a few other investigators, but not me. My name was always Rick or Richard. The name Richard Page was on my cards. The name "Dick" fits only with Tracy, Powell and Foran, but more often, it was synonymous with ass hole.

"Yes, sir, I'm a private investigator."

"I want you to find a man for me."

When he said that I was relieved, but not totally. I didn't have the time to work a heavy-dollar case like Prendergast's and do a search for Salvatore Trugante, but Trugante was not a man who would take "I'm too busy" for an answer. Worse yet, he wouldn't take "I can't find him" either.

"Who're you looking for?"

"You work with Alice. You find the bastard who knocked her up and you arrange for a meeting."

Uh-oh. "Does she have his name?"

"She won't tell me. If she will not tell you, it is up to you to find out. Can you do this for me?"

Even "I'll try" wouldn't be acceptable. "Yes, sir," I said. I was now committed to him more than to Prendergast.

Trugante told me to come to his house in Laurel Canyon tomorrow and I could talk to his daughter. Trugante's stooge gave me my gun back.

It was the first time I had ever been hired to arrange a shotgun wedding.

* * * *

I was almost a half-hour late getting to the Larabee. I didn't see Dixie Joy and I stood at the bar. A guy with a crewcut and a Hawaiian shirt made his way through the crowd and came straight at me.

"You Rick Page?" He was skinny and he hardly looked old enough to drink.

"Yeah, that's me."

"Dixie said I should give you this." He handed me a business size envelope.

"How'd you pick me out so quick?"

"You look like you might be carrying a gun."

"That simple?" It was not a way I wanted to look at the moment.

"Yes, sir. She says there's a note inside explaining everything."

"How do you know her?"

"Just friends. But I gotta get out of here."

"Hold on."

"Sorry."

He turned away quickly and started for the door. He was too far for me to grab and I didn't feel like chasing him until I checked the rest of the place out. I glanced at the crowd of maybe twenty people. Everyone seemed too busy to notice me. Even on a Tuesday, it was after-work pickup time.

I sat in my car and read the note that was scribbled on a folded piece of typing paper: "Afraid to wait, go to the Hollywood Vista Motel, ask for D. Jordan."

CHAPTER V

It looked like Dixie Joy was afraid of someone, so I made sure that nobody followed me. I parked on the street around the corner from the Hollywood Vista Motel.

The motel was not class, but it wasn't a dive either. The old guy in the office told me where D. Jordan's room was and I took the stairs to the second deck outside and to room 212. Just to be safe, I had my .38 in my hand before I knocked. Dixie peeked through the crack and she looked terrified. She quickly unhooked the chain, let me in, then looked both ways before she closed the door again.

"I am terribly sorry that I did not wait for you."

"Who are you afraid of? Trugante?"

"No. I am afraid of Mister Prendergast, I think. Somethin' is wrong."

I turned the chair away from the dressing table and straddled it. She sat at the foot of the bed and folded her hands in her lap. She was wearing the same skirt and blouse as when I saw her get out of the cab. *Zip-a-Dee-Doo-Dah* was playing low on the radio, but Miss Joy was not having a wonderful day.

"If he cannot get to her, he will come after *me*."

"Why?"

"He likes to play with people."

"Play?"

"It is not much fun for the people he plays with, but he does get his pleasure from it, I can tell you that – and sometimes, quite literally *his* pleasure."

Prendergast had more money than most movie moguls and he flashed it readily. Not only with the opulence of his house, but with little things, like offering to double my fee if I actually did bring his wife back to him. Apparently, he had used private eyes before and the results were not to his liking.

"Laura ran away because she was tired of being tortured – quite literally, tortured," Dixie said. "I knew it would happen. She thought she was being freed from bondage, but she was being sold into a worse kind of slavery."

"Who owns you?"

"No one *owns* me. I have a job. I was just ... accompanying someone that evenin'."

"You're a secretary."

"Yes, but he likes to drape me over his arm— Does that awful Tyree Prendergast know about me and where I am?"

"Miss Joy, the only things I know bad about Mister Prendergast are the things I'm hearing from you."

For at least a while, I would have to take everything she said with a boatload of salt. She had her own magic to weave. She was doing a good job of it, and I would listen, but I'd make my own judgments.

"Prendergast is insane!"

"But Laura married him?"

"She did not have a choice."

"Everybody has a choice. You can go home and start over or start over in another town. Nobody says you have to stay in L.A. She could have gone back to Cleveland after she lost her job at MGM. She chose to work for Cameron."

Dixie's cheeks flushed red and she looked into the mirror behind me. Her eyes were moving as if she was watching a scene or reading a billboard. Then she focused on me again.

"I have a choice, but Laura does not – not anymore."

"Are you running from Prendergast too?"

"No!"

"And your house on Doheny? You abandoned it?"

"It does not belong to me. Two other young ladies live there too, but it is not that kind of house. I should not have let you inside the doe-ah." She meant, "door," of course.

"You were expecting somebody when I came to the house on Doheny. Who?"

"I was expectin' no one."

"And why did you call me? Why did you leave a note for me to meet you here?"

"I want you to find Laura."

"I'm already doing that for Prendergast."

"But I don't want you to turn her over to him."

By calling her, I was pulled into an aspect of Laura being missing that was none of my business. But like I've always said, sometimes my brain gets challenged by other parts of my anatomy.

"I'm working for Prendergast. He's the one who's footing the bill," I said.

"How much is he paying you?"

"More than you can afford."

"Do you know how much I used to get for a couple of hours of intimate pleasure?"

"I only work for cash or good checks." I got up from the chair and turned it under the dresser. Her implication had gone straight to my brain. She was bartering. It was a bad play on her part. It would be even worse for me if I took her up on it.

"If you just stop looking for her, I would–"

"You've already made it quite clear what you'd do."

She rose from the bed and stepped toward me. She was smiling, but it wasn't working. If she had started off like that, she might have convinced me through my reflexes, but my brain was in control now. I never betray a client unless he does something wrong to me first or I slip up. So far, Prendergast hadn't done anything wrong and I didn't plan to slip up.

As Dixie drew closer, I got a whiff of her perfume. At another time in such close confines, the scent might have helped convince me to betray a client, but she had already warned me and I was on guard.

"Don't you care?" she said.

"No."

She put her hand behind my head. I put both of my palms on her shoulders and forced her away.

"Please?" she asked.

"Sorry."

"At least keep him from killin' her?"

"Keep who from killing her?"

"Prendergast." She put her hands on her hips and pouted. "You don't believe me. You don't believe anythin' I'm tellin' you."

"Not a word," I said.

"Please?"

I had already reached for the door. She came behind me. She put her hands on my shoulders and pressed her face and breasts against my back. She had fired the furnace inside me, but I had the control I needed for now.

"At least keep me and Laura from gettin' killed."

"I'll take you to Union Station. You can take a train to anyplace you want to go, but I have to find Laura and take her to Prendergast first."

"That won't help her, I swear."

"She could be in Cleveland by now," I said. It was time to get out of there before I started to make deals that I'd regret.

"Please," she said when I stepped onto the motel deck.

Please is no argument to a man who already knew you were manipulating him – it's hardly ever an argument to anything else either.

* * * *

I had kept Tyree Prendergast waiting too long. Instead of calling him, I went to his house off Benedict Canyon. I followed a brand new Cadillac most of the way up. It turned into Prendergast's Estate about a hundred yards ahead of me and was inside before I reached the closing gate.

I got out of my car just in time to see the Caddie go into the six-car carriage house. I pressed the intercom and I identified myself. Somebody did whatever magic it took and the ornate, wrought iron gates unlocked for me and swung open.

Five minutes later, Prendergast's butler led me into the large living room. The fifty-foot cube was big enough to be a ballroom. It had three marble walls and one of glass. There were chandeliers of rectangular cut crystal that hung from four places in the ceiling.

* * * *

Earlier today, I had seen the first tee and last green of his private golf course through the glass. Tonight, the windows reflected the interior of the room with its classic Roman furniture, its Persian rugs, and paintings by artists whose work I knew by whose names I didn't.

"Is there something I can get you, sir?" said the butler.

"Nothing," I said.

Prendergast flicked his wrist, ushering away the smallish butler.

While some of us were leaving our jobs and going overseas, others were working at home in factories to support us. People like Prendergast were designing and building airplanes and ships and weapons that helped us win the war. At the same time, they were building elaborate and comfortable cathedrals of living to enjoy the wealth that war was giving them.

Prendergast did not speak until the butler was out of the room. "Why didn't you call me back immediately?"

"Because I was trying to find your wife."

"And did you?" Ty Prendergast was taller than I was, with a full head of gray hair, and a protruding lower lip that kept him from being handsome.

"I've had some luck, but it's not enough to work with yet. I have a lot more questions to ask, a lot more people to talk to."

"I want to know everything that you know."

"Not possible. I explained that when we started."

"What if I were to stop payment on that check I gave you this morning?"

"Then you'd start all over with another private detective and you'd be right back to the beginning. I have leads and I'll follow them up."

"Do you know where she is?"

"If I knew where she was, I'd have her. It's only leads so far. That's why I told you I'd give you a report only once a week."

"When the advance has run out?"

"A week's advance can last more than a week. I've hardly put a dent in it. Some people say they saw her. I'm still verifying the stories."

"Who? Where?"

"Instead of telling you, I'm going to ask you some questions. Where did you meet your wife?"

"That is none of your *God* damned business."

"Is it safe to say that it wasn't at a church social?"

The red faded from his cheeks just a bit. "It's safe to say that. Yes."

"I've tracked her along some pretty drastic lines and to some pretty unsavory people. Some of it is information you should have given me to begin with. I'll let it go at that."

"You tracked her to where?"

"That's all I'm saying. We went over this when I came to you this morning. The plan is that I let you know how I'm doing, not what I'm doing. The worst thing in a case like this is if you go poking around yourself. Before we know it, we're accusing each other and you still won't find your wife."

"Suppose I hire another detective to help you?"

"I don't work that way. He'll just screw up what I'm already doing. This is not easy, Mister Prendergast. It is very possible that your wife left entirely on her own accord."

"Will I get her back safely?" He ignored what I said.

"Maybe the best I'll be able to do is to get her to talk to you. Why do you emphasize the 'safely' part? Do you know something that you're not telling me?"

"A few things."

"Like the fact that she was a prostitute?"

Prendergast started to come out of his chair, but he slumped back. The word "yes" barely hissed through his teeth and he stared at a space between my feet.

"There's a chance that I'll get her back safely." I said it casually and it sounded like a guarantee, but not even the FBI can guarantee the safety of a missing person. "Have you had any ransom notes yet?"

"No. And I don't expect any. Whoever took her, took her for reasons other than ransom."

He told me the same thing this morning with the implication that she was so beautiful and so unbelievably wonderful that almost any man would want her for himself. No one would ever dream of holding her for ransom.

"You haven't reported this to the police yet, right?" I said.

"You told me not to."

"Good. If the radio and newspapers announce that Tyree Prendergast's wife has gone missing, you'll have more ransom notes than you have money to cover."

"You are working exclusively on this case, are you not?"

"Yes." It would be the truth until tomorrow morning when I would go and speak to Salvatore Trugante and his daughter.

"When someone works for me, I expect total loyalty."

"I give that to every client."

"Which means?"

"I work for you like I work for anybody else. You get my full attention while I'm working on your case. If I gave some clients more attention than the others, I would soon have no clients at all." I should have crossed my fingers at the lie.

"If you betray me, you still might have no other clients – not if you want to work in Los Angeles."

"I don't do well under threats."

"Then learn."

"No, I don't think so. And you don't want me to, not if you really want to find your wife."

"What do you mean not if I *really* want to find her?"

"I mean that you're telling me things and paying me money, but I don't see the slightest hint that you're upset about her being missing."

"I assure you that I *do* want her back." He had a way of emphasizing words to make sure I understood, but this time, I thought the meaning was negative. He wanted to find her, but did he still didn't seem to care about her.

"I've been in the business of making money for a long time," Prendergast continued. "And I've heard all kinds of stories. It sounds as if you might be trying to soften me up for something. Maybe because you can't find her. Or *won't* find her."

"I do a job. I don't play games. If you think that's the case, we can call it quits right now."

He glared with his hard gray eyes that might drill holes in someone else's resolve, but not mine. I did not break eye contact.

"Where was she seen?"

"No, sir."

"I'll pay you additional for–"

"No interim reports. It works better. You have to trust me. I have leads about where she might have been, but the odds are good that she's not there anymore. If you or somebody else goes poking around behind me, we'll stumble all over each other and maybe blow the whole thing."

"You already handed me that bullshit story."

"Let's call it 'bullshit' for emphasis. I have the impression from the message I was given that you might know something new. Did you get a call?" I asked him.

"Nothing. I'll give you the total amount of the advance if you will you tell me what you have so far."

"Easy enough. I can agree to that. I'll give you the information and walk out of here. It's easy money for me, but it's not the smart for you – not if you want to find her."

He looked beyond me to the wall of glass. For a moment, I thought he was looking at his own reflection, but I saw his image in the mirror on the wall facing me. He was staring at me through a double reflection and over a long distance, and he was judging me.

I rose from my chair. "My time here is costing you money. I think it might better be spent on the street."

"I don't expect to run out of money."

"I don't suppose you would, but with your permission, I would like to get back to work."

"Get out."

"I'll give you a detailed report a week from today. By then, I will either have found her or you can make some other arrangement."

"Other arrangement? I thought you guaranteed–"

"I didn't guarantee anything and you know it. I've learned the positive approach is the best approach. I *do* expect to find your wife."

"Don't play games with me either, Mister Page."

"I'll stop when you stop," I said and started for the front door.

"Where do you think you're going?"

"I'm sure your butler will get to the door before I do."

The more money a client had, the rougher I treated him. They didn't like it, but it taught them respect they might not have otherwise. Either that or they fired me and that was okay, too.

Somebody like Trugante was a different story. I didn't know Trugante except by rumor. No matter how much money he had, I was unlikely to treat him the way I had just treated Prendergast.

CHAPTER VI

Benedict Canyon, where I had just been, was the kind of place where they might stop you because you happened to be driving a Ford, so when the car behind me flashed its lights off and on, I pulled to the side of the road and waited. I expected a burly cop from Beverly Hills to get out and come to my car. Instead, it just waited behind me.

As a private eye, you set a number of personal rules. One of mine was to stop when I thought it was a cop, not to stop when I didn't, and to have my gun ready in case I was wrong. Nobody got out of the car behind me, so I pulled away.

"Hey!" somebody shouted. It was a female voice.

I was already moving when I realized it was Dixie Joy in her Pontiac, but it didn't keep me from driving on. I did not try to lose her, and she followed me all the way to the Hollywood Vista Motel. When I stopped on the street, she stopped behind me and jumped out.

"Why you runnin' away?"

"This is where you live, right?" I gestured.

"Temporarily. Would you like to come in?"

"No matter what happens in there, it's not a deal."

"Well, you can come on in just for the awful hell of it."

How could I refuse?

She put her new Pontiac on the lot. I parked on the street and followed her to room 212. When I stepped inside, she bolted the door and attached the chain. I put my hat on the dressing table.

The bed was already turned down, and sounds of the old Glenn Miller Orchestra were easing from the radio. She still wore the blouse, the skirt and the patent leather belt. She sat on the edge of the bed and looked up at me. With her terrible baby-blue eyes, she launched into a full seductive attack.

Most women make emotional commitments to sex. Some men do too, but I don't, because I know I can't keep them. A lot of men can lie or fool themselves. I can always open a nice package – unless I hear ticking. I was keeping my ears keen to this one.

I pulled a chair from under the dressing table, sat in front of her and held her hands. I looked straight into her eyes.

"No matter what we do here, it won't be a trade for anything," I said.

"Did you find Laura?"

"No."

"Do you think you will?"

"Probably."

"And for my sake, will you keep her from him?"

"No."

"No matter what you learn? No matter what I tell you about him?"

I shook my head, and she looked down at her hands. Her nails were well manicured, her hair was set in waves but loose and the toes of her pumps were turned in. Her entire demeanor was like a girl half her age. It was as much an act as it was with any teenager, but an act that she considered necessary.

"Will you protect her?"

"Yes," I said.

"Okay."

She looked up from under her brow and smiled. It was a weak smile, but it was all she could muster at the moment.

"You do know what it was that I used to do for a livin'."

"Yeah."

She stood and I looked up at her. She unbuckled the patented leather belt as she did before. This time, she tossed it to the floor on the other side of the bed.

"No deals," I said.

"I know."

She undid the buttons one at a time and slipped out of her blouse. She unhooked her skirt and lowered it along with her half-slip, holding them with one hand and holding my shoulder with the other. She stepped out of them and folded them on the dresser. Her wasp-waisted corset cinched her tightly. She put one foot at a time on the edge of the bed, and unhooked her hose from the garter suspenders that were connected her corset. She sat and rolled her stockings, one at a time. She threw them against the mirror behind my head as if she intended to hit me. Then she smiled broadly.

I wanted to tell her again that there were no deals, but she understood by now.

"Why are you doing this?" I asked.

"Because I want to."

"Me too."

"Of course you do, you *are* a man. All men *want* to." She stood, turned her back to me and glanced over her shoulder like a woman on a pin-up calendar. "Would you be so kind as to unhook me?"

I knew that women hooked these things in the front then turned the whole business around, but I never understood how they fingered the hooks. It was bad enough getting them undone.

"You don't have to do this," I said.

"Oh you just shut up," she said.

Her unrestrained body was not very different from what she had squeezed into her corset. She gathered the whole business in front of her, carried it to dresser and folded it all. I would have stopped her long ago and wrapped my arms around her, but I wanted to see the routine. She was good. She had to be when she worked for Michael Cameron. Now it had become habit.

She came back wearing a camisole with nothing but her panties underneath. Her breasts were firm, but not large, and her nipples pushed against the nylon, showing her interest.

"Are you goin' to do this with your clothes on?" she asked.

"Sometimes I do," I said and she knew I was teasing.

Something was going on inside me that I didn't understand. I knew who this woman was and what she had been. I could have ripped off her panties, slammed her against the nearest wall, and plunged into her. It would take away the tension that had built inside me, but it wouldn't satisfy me. That kind of sex usually didn't, unless I was angry, but I wanted to see her again.

I stood.

I wanted to know where she was from and how she got to be she was now. I almost chuckled, because I wanted to know if she could really type and take shorthand and if her accent had ever been real.

She unbuckled me, unzipped me, held me there with one hand and put her other behind my head. She kissed me, but it was not just a kiss, it was a routine. She nibbled my lips, parted them and slipped just the tip of her tongue to mine. The kiss was slow and soft and I tasted her lipstick. I heard her breath, I smelled her perfume. I knew she was manipulating me, not only with her hands and her lips, but she was turning my own thoughts against me.

She rolled her panties to the floor and looked up at me with those eyes.

"Please find her," she whispered as she stood. She gripped my arms and rolled back onto the bed with me on top of her.

"I will," I said. I wanted it to be a promise because I wanted Laura to be okay, but I would still have to give her to Prendergast.

"This very well might be more fun than I had hoped," she said.

"Yeah," I said.

"Shhh."

I kissed her again and moved into position. I knew that she was trying to buy something with her body, but it made no difference. I liked her and it was nice, very nice. I liked her persistence. Rustles, sighs, nips, kisses on every part of her body and on every part of mine that wasn't still covered.

"Oh, Lordy," she said at the end.

"Yeah," I said.

"Next time we'll do it when you have no clothes," she said, but what happened was her choice, wholly her choice. I was just along for the pleasure of it. I'd bet she was worth a lot of dollars, but they were damn sure dollars I didn't have.

Afterward, she lay still while I smoked a cigarette.

"Please don't turn her back to him."

"I have no choice," I said.

"Please?"

"I told you we weren't making a deal."

"I was just hopin'."

She followed me to the door. She gave me one last kiss and I liked it.

"Call me when you settle in someplace," I said.

"I'm settled here for a while."

I could have gotten into a conversation about why, but I didn't feel like sorting out lies. I would rather end on the upbeat.

* * * *

It was almost one in the morning when I left the Hollywood Vista. It was not the best route to my apartment, but I went down to Hollywood Boulevard and drove past the Roosevelt Hotel. People were coming out of the bars. I was watching them and musing at their existence as I often mused about my own. As I waited for the light at Highland Avenue, a blonde hurried between my car and the one in front of me. She was trying to get across Hollywood Boulevard among the drunks and the drunken drivers. She looked panicked and damn it, she looked like Laura Prendergast!

"Laura!" I called.

I looked to see if anyone was chasing her. If they were, I didn't see them. She was on the other side of Hollywood Boulevard now and she had slowed to a fast walk.

I drove slowly, trying to keep up with her and the driver in the car behind me beeped his horn.

"Laura," I called again.

She stopped, looked both ways and crossed through a break in the traffic. She leaned over to see into the car. Her face was good, but her flesh was pale. Her eyes looked like bubbling death.

"Who are you?"

"Somebody who's looking for you."

"Why are you looking for me?" she said. She looked over her shoulder, then forced a smile at me.

I didn't want her to embarrass herself further, so I said, "Your husband wants you home."

It was the exact wrong thing to say, but the words came out before I thought. It's an old habit that I've been trying to break.

Her mouth dropped open. She stood upright and hurried across the street. A taxi veered around her.

I pulled to a space at a fireplug. The guy who had been behind me leaned on his horn as I opened the door and got out. I would have started after her, but I lost her. I didn't even know which direction she went. I stood against my car, looking both ways on Hollywood Boulevard for the telltale head-bob of someone pushing through a crowd, but I didn't see it. I crossed to the sidewalk on the other side of the street, but I still couldn't find her.

At least she was alive, I thought. I rarely lose a subject when I'm that close, but I did lose her.

"Damn it!" It was my own fault. I spoke too soon.

"Hi," said another blonde. She took me by the arm.

"Hi, yourself," I snapped at her.

She released my arm, backed up, and hurried away.

I thought about the murder of the taxi driver on the lot behind my office. Unless Sandiri decided to do something about it, the police would handle it as a routine murder and robbery that they would attribute to somebody who needed to be put away for a while.

CHAPTER VII

Marco Sandiri knew my habits and he arrived at the parking lot behind my office at nine in the morning just as I did. He was built square, with broad shoulders, but he was not terribly tall. He was one of the toughest cops I ever met and one of the hardest working.

"I did some more on that crap you gave me yesterday," he said as he followed my up to my office. I unlocked the door and let him in.

"Stinks in here," Sandiri said. He was one of those rare cops who didn't smoke, and he hated the smell of it. I put my hat on the clothes tree. Then I went to the window and opened it.

"What crap did I give you yesterday?"

"We checked the drivers log. He didn't go anyplace near Misty Crest."

"I know what his log said, but he told me he did. He could've high-flagged from the Roosevelt and come right back. He told me about it quick so the dispatcher wouldn't catch on."

"What bothers me is that right after you talked to him, he got robbed and skunked. I want to know where you got the information about the pickup."

"You want my sources?"

"I'll treat them kindly. Might even slip them a buck or two."

"Little Georgie."

I lied because I wanted to protect Dixie Joy until I got more information from her. Once the cops had her as a major witness, there was no telling how many lies she might spit out.

"Little Georgie, huh? Some source."

"He gives good reads," I said.

Sandiri walked to the window and looked across the street as if he wanted to know what was playing at the Palladium. I figured he was deciding how hard to come down on me.

"Did you find your blonde yet?"

"Not yet."

"I tried a couple of other houses on Misty Crest, nobody saw or heard anybody coming in late Saturday night."

"Wouldn't be a first time?"

"That's what I thought. I pushed, but nobody's budging. It was like they're afraid. Prendergast hasn't reported his wife missing yet. I gave him a call."

"Any luck?" I asked.

"His butler said that he was not in and when I asked about the missus he said that she's out of town for a few weeks. Do you think I should push him?"

"You're asking me for advice about that? I'm still working for Prendergast."

"She's gonna turn up dead, you know?"

"I don't think so," I said.

"Cabbie's dead for knowing too much. That's a sign. I did some checking on Prendergast. He made nice airplanes, but he's not a very nice guy. How'd he get your name?"

"Yellow pages, but that's what the all say."

"And you didn't push for more?"

"When somebody as rich as him offers me a week's work at double per diem, I don't question him on the trivials, and I don't accuse him of murder unless I think he did one. It's better for business. I'm sure he got me from a reliable source."

"Some other rich crook, huh?"

"Is he a crook?"

"Figure of speech. Cabbie had his throat slit."

I huffed and slumped in my chair. "Sounds like a mob hit, but which mob?" L.A. was full of mobs.

"Mob would've been a garrote or a bullet. You gonna tell me everything you know or am I going to have to sweat it out of you?"

He was kidding, of course. He knew he'd never sweat anything out of me, but he would put me through hell in an interrogation room if he thought it necessary to get the whole story.

I stared out the window at the wood-square design over the marquee of the Palladium. I hadn't been there since I saw Gene Krupa when I first came home from the war. Benny Goodman wasn't with him, but he still did a hell of a drum solo with *Sing, Sing, Sing*.

What kept me from going back was a combination of being too busy, not having enough money and having nobody to go with. When I was working, I had money. When I wasn't working, I was afraid to spend it. A lousy ninety-two cents, but I didn't like going alone. I wondered if a girl like Dixie Joy would consider going the Palladium sometime.

"Are you with me here, Rick?"

"Pardon?"

"What are you thinking about?"

"The missing wife. Maybe I'd better tell you everything."

"Maybe you'd better."

This time I told him about everything I knew including story of the little guy in the bowler and the convention of inventors for movie gimmicks at the Roosevelt on Saturday night. I told him that Michael Cameron provided the girls.

"Which means that I have to lay off – at least that aspect of it," he said.

"Why?"

"Like you said, which mob? Unfortunately, a couple of them have enough pull to–"

He cut himself off. He didn't think that anything he told me would go any further, but he couldn't trust me not to let something slip.

"I understand," I said.

I knew that there were at least two rings of upper echelon cops who were skimming gravy from a lot of full caldrons. Sandiri was never in on the take, which was why his lieutenant used to be his junior partner.

"I didn't like the log. It was too neat, too precise, like an accountant did it," I said.

"Or a dispatcher fudging the books. I wanted to see if the dispatch guy would tell me himself, but he didn't. I don't like him either. But you're missing the obvious – your missing lady and the cabbie are connected."

"Really?"

"Don't be a smart aleck."

I decided not to tell him about spending a few hours last night with Dixie Joy, but I did tell him about seeing Laura Prendergast on the street.

"Are you sure it was her?"

"She was running from something. Then I said the wrong thing and she ran from me."

"There are a lot of blondes in L.A. and they're all either running from something or after something."

I remembered her face, her expression and her fear. "It was her all right."

"Walking Hollywood Boulevard at one in the morning, huh? And why do you think she doesn't want to go back to her husband? Doesn't he pay her enough?"

"That's where something's screwed up. I don't quite buy the stories I'm hearing."

"You know, Rick, there's not a private eye in L.A. that I can talk to like you. You leave out just enough to make it interesting."

"Like what?"

"Like what stories are you hearing? And who from?"

"You have most of it. You'll get it all sooner or later. What do you know about Salvatore Trugante?"

Sandiri sat back. "You think he's got something to do with this?"

"It's something else I'm working on." I told him about Trugante's daughter.

"I wouldn't mess with Trugante if I were you."

"I don't have much of a choice. What racket is he in?" I wanted to hear more about it.

"High class whore houses."

"Just like Cameron?"

"Cameron works for him. Either that or Cameron pays him some kind of protection. It could all connect with–"

"The city fathers."

"The city fathers are mothers. They'll hook up with anybody who will roll a couple thou their way every once in a while."

"Do you realize how much 'half' information you give me?" I said.

"Yeah, just about as much as you give me. You follow up on that Cameron-Trugante thing. I'll do the same," he said.

"So you can tell me to lay off?"

"If it comes to that."

We were finished and our timing was perfect. I was due at the house of Salvatore Trugante in a half-hour.

* * * *

Beverly Hills has a police force that is separate from Los Angeles County and there was less governmental corruption, so people who chose to live and operate illegally did it someplace else. That was why Michael Cameron chose The Tower in West Hollywood for his headquarters and Salvatore Trugante chose to work out of his home in Laurel Canyon within a mile of Hollywood Boulevard. Sandiri told me that none of Trugante's "houses" were in Beverly Hills. Trugante had learned on the streets. I heard that Cameron had to go to Princeton to sharpen his business sense, but he had the same street education some of the rest of us had.

The gates at the Trugante Estate were not electronically operated like Prendergast's. They had a mug in a box who made sure that only the proper undesirables were permitted to enter. I fell into that category, but first I had to prove I was the right guy.

"You got a driver's license?" the mug said.

I showed it to him. He asked for my birth date, like I was a kid trying to get into a bar illegally.

"First building after the U-turn. That's the office," he said. I followed his directions except that there were four U-turns up one side of the Canyon wall before I came to any buildings.

The first building turned out to be the ground floor of what looked like a five-story house that was also cut into the wall. The top floor seemed to be all glass. Another building looked like a three-car garage with a second story. A man dressed in a silver suit opened the door and patted me down. He was not the butler.

He asked permission to hold my .38 and the .22 automatic that I had in my ankle holster.

"Absolutely."

"You'll get them back when you leave."

"Thanks."

"I am so sorry for the formality, Mister Page," Dixie Joy said as she rose from her chair behind the receptionist desk.

I frowned.

"A girl just has to make a living," she said. "You are here for Mister Trugante. Is that correct?"

"Yeah."

She wore a black dress that would have looked good on anybody and a pair of oversized glasses that magnified the circles under her eyes. She had a typewriter at her desk and she probably took shorthand, so that part of her personal legend seemed to check out. She stepped through to another office and held the door open for me.

I thought she said "Good luck" under her breath. I quickly translated what I thought I heard to what I actually heard, and I chuckled.

Trugante had just slipped into his suit jacket. He offered his hand. "Good to see you could make it," he said, as if I had a choice. Today's toupee had a better fit than the one he wore last night.

He gestured for me to sit in a chair that was manufactured to make anyone feel comfortable and overconfident. He was smart.

"I want you to see my daughter in a minute or two, but I want you to understand what you are allowed to do and what you are not allowed to do."

I nodded. I noticed that the light on his desk intercom was on, which meant that someone else might be listening to our conversation. I gestured to the light and he waved down my hand.

"What you are supposed to do when you talk to my Alice, is compliment her, smile, wait on her even, but find out what you can about this lowly son of a bitch who got her pregnant. What you are not allowed to do is to have any kind of carnal relations with her. Others?" He shrugged. I think he was talking about Dixie and I wondered how he knew about that.

"Understood," I said.

Last night, when he had me in the back of his limousine, he seemed like any other thug I had ever dealt with. Today, behind his large desk and with his fingers pressed against each other steeple style, he was like a businessman. His words seemed very precisely selected, yet his cadence was a bit awkward and choppy. I wondered if he had learned the language from teachers who taught him precision in pronunciation or if it was all his own doing.

"I say that, Mister Page, because I suspect that she will try to throw her slightly pregnant body at you at every opportunity she gets. She has declined to tell me who is this bastard. You are to coax it out of her if you can. But you may use other resources if she will not talk to you."

It sounded impossible, but I nodded.

"We are looking for the fellow who did the knock up, and I have three possible names. Well, two since you have been eliminated as the father. It will now be up to you to help me determine who the father should be."

"Shouldn't a doctor–"

"I did not say it is up to you to determine who the father *is*, but who the father *should* be. Frankly, from what little I have seen and what I have heard, I could tolerate you as a son-in-law. But your relations are too far in the past and you would not be fooled into believing that it is your child."

"Wouldn't be a good idea for Alice to–"

"If I let her choose, she will choose a bum."

"The two names that you'll give me, who–"

"They are both bums. What you are to decide is which is the least of whatever bums you find. Or which is the best, if it so happens that a likely father is not a bum. I want you to choose a person who, with my guidance perhaps, might make not only a suitable husband for my Alice, but a man who might work in my organization. Do you understand?"

"Yes, sir."

I understood, but it sounded like a dumb idea, especially since he had an obsession that whoever the father was must be a "bum." It was a word that seemed to obsess him.

The logical thing, I thought, was for me to find the true father and to see if the natural love that he might have for a child would spread back to Alice herself – if he was not already in love with her. She was attractive and she had her good qualities. Unfortunately, my best recollection was that she was terribly spoiled and she expected adulation out of her lovers.

"I have the names, which I will give you after you have a quiet conversation and explain to her that you will be helping me find the father of her child."

"Doesn't she know who it is?"

"She refuses to say. Now, I will have Miss Dixie take you to the pool where Alice suns herself from dawn until dusk."

"Yes, sir."

"Miss Dixie!" he called.

In a few seconds the door opened. "If you do not mind, would you take Mister Page to the pool and introduce, reintroduce him to Alice."

"Yes, sir," she said.

We went out of his office, down a narrow corridor, and stopped at an elevator that was already open.

"You look good this morning, considering," I said.

"So do you – considerin'."

She hit the button. The elevator jerked, then started to move.

"I saw–"

Dixie brought her finger to her lips then did a little circle motion with it while she looked around the ceiling, indicating that there might be ears in the elevator. Before we reached the fifth and top floor, she handed me a neatly torn piece of typing paper on which she had printed a phone number and an address on Misty Crest Road. Next to the number, she had printed the words *MINE, DAYTIME* in all capital letters. Next to the address was *NOT MINE*.

"Right this way, Mister Page," she said.

We stepped into a greenhouse and solarium that must be at the very top of the canyon wall. In the middle was a long and narrow pool. In planters around the pool and against the glass, there were more kinds of plants and flowers than I could identify with a botanical guidebook, but roses predominated.

Alice Trugante, who I had known as Alice Smith, sat upright on a chaise, reading. She wore a one-piece red bathing suit, with the upper part tied behind her neck. She was a blonde when I knew her and she was even blonder now. The sun through the glass might have caused that, but it was more likely that the almost white-blonde hair had come from a bottle. Her pregnancy didn't show yet.

When we had stepped from the elevator, her eyes returned to pages of the book. As we approached, she held up her hand for silence and continued to read. When I first met her, she was heavily made up and I misjudged her age. From what I saw now, she was maybe twenty.

After about a minute of irritating both Dixie and me, she closed her book and looked up.

"How good to see you again," she said.

"Likewise."

"You can leave us."

"Yes, ma'am," Dixie said and she went back to the elevator.

"Has Papa told you what your job is?"

"I'd like to hear it from you."

"It's very simple. You go to Central Casting and find me a husband. That should be easy enough."

I sat on the chaise next to hers with my feet planted firmly on the black and white tiles. A swimming pool was visible on the other side of a wall of plants and planters.

"That's the smart Alice version. What's the real story?"

As if from a loud speaker, I heard Sal Trugante's voice from the corner of the solarium. "You tell the man what he wants to know!"

"Yes, Papa, but please turn off the loud speaker."

CHAPTER VIII

"You're not applying for the husband job are you?"

Alice Trugante grinned and strolled to the round, glass-top table in the corner. She reached over, flicked off the switch on the intercom system and strolled back in my direction. She was assessing me. I hoped it was not as a future husband, but you could never be sure with a girl who always got her own way.

"Not for that job," I said.

I pitied any man who had to marry her. She would put him through hell and he would probably end up being fed to the sharks anyway.

"I do not want a husband, Mister Page – if that's you're real name?"

"The same name I gave you when we met."

"So many men give a phony name, but I always get the right name in the end."

"You mean like 'Smith?'"

"Smith was the name I was going to use in the movies."

Alice was tiny and quite attractive. I could easily see her as an actress. Acting was probably something she had done all her life, first getting everything she wanted from Papa, then almost anything from most other men.

"Who are the candidates?" I asked.

"It's not an election."

"What is it then?"

She huffed. "You still don't like me, do you?"

"I don't have to like you. I just have to do the job for you."

"You are not doing the job for me, you are doing it for Papa." She chuckled. "You must admit that two bodybuilders seems like a better deal for a girl than a little old private detective. Well, you are not that little, although you are old. What are you now, forty?"

"Thirty-two. You don't look very pregnant."

"Seven weeks."

"And you already told your father?"

"He is a perceptive man, and when he asks a question that I choose to answer, I don't lie to him. If I don't answer, he figures out the truth anyway."

"He gave me the names of two prospective husbands."

"Only two? I'd think that he would have every eligible bachelor in Los Angeles on his list – especially if they had money, power, or influence. But then, Papa has enough of that on his own, doesn't he?"

"Who are the potential fathers?"

"Papa knows about *three*. He knows about you – don't look at me that way – that leaves two other possibilities, but don't expect to get the names from me."

"I don't think you are nearly as promiscuous as you pretend to be and–"

"The two bodybuilders didn't convince you?" She had a point.

"Do *you* know who the father is?"

She went misty and stared through the glass to the higher peak on the other side of Laurel Canyon.

"What is it?"

"Nothing."

When the word "nothing" comes as a response, there is often something big not far behind, or something that is about to be covered up. I waited a few seconds.

"Can you tell me about it?" I said.

"It was nothing, really."

It was something, but I think she locked herself into keeping it a secret for now.

"A married man, I'll bet," I said.

"You bet wrong. So how much do you owe me?"

She was always coy, and she always made jokes, often about things that were not at all funny.

"You don't understand what this is really all about do you?" she asked.

"I'm supposed to find you a suitable husband."

"Not a suitable husband, not even the real father of my child, but a man who will make me a widow very quickly. You don't understand Papa. He does not see me as his wild I-don't-give-a-damn daughter. He sees me as his innocent little girl who was dragged off to wickedness by all those awful men who seduced her. The weakness, Rick, is not in sweet, innocent little Alice but in those who seduce her. Even now, Papa thinks I'm too young to make my own decisions. People like you have to make them for me."

"People like me?"

"Yes, detectives, henchmen, torpedoes. You must know that anyone who has ever allowed themselves to be seduced by me is guilty in Papa's eyes. He would never believe that I could seduce – or practically ask for it the way I did with you. You absolutely must have seen what an innocent little girl I was."

She fluttered her lashes and twisted the tip of her index finger into an imaginary dimple at her chin.

"Papa wants a scapegoat, a big wedding, and an unfortunate accident. He wants you to choose who the deceased will be."

"It was an older man who started you off, wasn't it?"

"Older? How much older?" She was playing with me.

"Maybe twice your age? When did it start?"

"It started before the war, but let's drop that angle, shall we? I'm not real keen on gouging my old wounds."

Whatever she was hiding was important to her, but I didn't think that it had anything to do who was the father of her unborn child.

"Give me the names of the bodybuilders?"

"No!" She said it sharply and she laughed. "Can you imagine what would happen if I told him *that* story? He'd accuse them of gang rape and cut them up in little pieces. You shouldn't fret about that. I left you not for two men, but for two gorgeous bodies. As for their performance – it left a lot to be desired. Quite a bit in fact. I tried to call you to apologize."

She had left three messages, and I chose not to call her back, because after only two weeks I was tired of her me-me-me attitude. The bodybuilders had verified a promiscuity that I already suspected. She was the female version of many men I knew. Instead of "wham, bam, thank you, ma'am," it was "lick fur, thank you, sir." She actually used that phrase in describing other men to me. She knew all the techniques that came over after the war and she knew what she wanted in return.

"How old were you?" I asked.

"Are you going to give a full report to Papa? Do you want the name of every man I ever fucked?" She threw me with that. The word coming from an ex-prostitute like Dixie made sense, but coming from a girl who was not yet old enough to vote? Well, maybe I was getting too old.

"I'm going to check out the names your father gave me and see who deserves you."

"Do you mean see who deserves to die?"

"Nothing like that."

"I was fourteen," she said and she bit her lips. "And I was still thinking about Rhett Butler carrying Scarlet up the stairs."

"Early start," I said.

"But most girls start with guys their own age."

"Yeah," I said.

There were tears in her eyes. I had hit on something that I didn't expect, and she didn't want to go into it. I was sure she was hiding an important name, but whoever he was, he might not be the father of her child.

* * * *

The address that Dixie Joy gave me on Misty Crest was at the end of the road and on top of the hill. When I looked at the number, I saw that it had the same digits that the cab driver gave me, but they were transposed. It and the house next door seemed to be vacant. From the porch, I could see down the houses and into Hollywood. When I pressed the button, I heard no chime, so I knocked and waited.

I knocked a second time and finished my Lucky Strike. I fieldstripped it, rolled the paper into a little ball and flicked the paper into the street. I rubbed out the ashes on the porch with my shoe and tried the door. It was open and the place was empty. There was no furniture inside.

I walked across the hardwood floor of the living room and dining room to the picture window that overlooked the Hollywood Bowl. I wondered if they could hear the music from here.

I flicked wall switches, but there was no power. There was no furniture in the bedrooms and no clothes in the closets. The floors had been swept at sometime in the past, but there were male and female footprints through a new layer of dust. There was nothing in the kitchen cabinets or drawers except a box of stick matches. There were no telephones in any of the rooms.

I went down the stairs to the basement, where light crept in from small windows high on the wall. There was no direct sunlight and no shadows, but something big hung by all fours in the middle of the room. For a moment, I thought it was a deer.

In a few seconds, the dark became gray in the faint light, and I recognized that triangular shape that hung from the ceiling was not a deer, but a woman's body. Her wrists and ankles were lashed together over a hook that came from the ceiling. Her naked belly sagged, her head drooped and her blonde hair hung in her face.

It made me sick, but I moved closer.

I went down to one knee and angled blonde hair away from her face with my sleeve. I had found Laura Prendergast, missing since last week, seen on Saturday night and again last night.

And now this.

It was full-tilt sadism. If I figured it right, based on the angle and placement of the body, sex was involved. I did not look for the telltale

44

cuts or bruises in the dark, but I was sure they would be there. I felt for a pulse under her jaw, but there was none.

I drove all the way to a pharmacy on La Brea where I called Sandiri. When I couldn't get through, I called the Hollywood Precinct. I gave them the address and told them there was a body in the basement of the house.

"Can I have your name?" the desk sergeant asked politely.

I hung up without replying.

CHAPTER IX

It's not easy to be blasé about death, even after you've seen missing limbs, torn flesh and exposed organs in combat. When you see tabloid photos of the Black Dahlia sliced in half as if by a ripsaw and displayed with her legs spread and her arms raised in surrender you understand that there are all kinds of death and all kinds of sick people dishing it out.

Laura Prendergast was not cut in half like the Dahlia, but she was hog-tied and hung by ropes on a hook. She was raped, tortured and murdered. Whoever did it had inflicted horrible pain in a cruel and vicious manner. I didn't know how, but I would get the sick son of a bitch who had so much fun with Laura in her final hours.

I did not to go to Prendergast. Instead, I went to my office and called Dixie Joy at the new number she gave me. It was just a few digits off Trugante's phone number and I figured it was her personal office number.

"Where did you get the address you gave me?"

"Have you talked to her yet?"

"No. Where did you get the address?"

Dixie did not whisper, but she talked in low tones. "Laura called last night and said somebody tried to take her home to her husband, but she said somebody else was after her too."

"Who?"

"She didn't say, but she gave me a description of the fella that tried to take her to Ty. That was you. I told her you were all right, but she said she was going to a place where she thought it was safe. That was the address she gave me. She said she had better chance with Ty than with the other boll shit that was going on."

"What other bullshit?"

"Somebody at the party put her in touch with some movie people from back east. She said they were weird."

"Little guy in the bowler hat?"

"She didn't say, but she said that they were into weird sexual activity. They liked to pinch and to bite, she said. She didn't like that, and she didn't like them because she kept thinkin' of that Dahlia gal the newspapers are all talkin' about."

"And she went back to them?"

"She was trying to get away! She said she would be safe at that place at the address I gave you."

"Safe, huh?"

"That's what she said."

I thought about it for half-a-second and decided not to tell her that Laura was dead. "How long is this number going to be good for?"

"In the daytime as long as I am still working for Mister Trugante, and that should be for a long while yet."

I already had her number at the Hollywood Vista. "Are you working on your own now? Or are you back working for Cameron?"

She hesitated, then sounded like she was speaking through clenched teeth. "I am not *workin'* for anyone in the way that you suggest. I am *workin'* for Mister Trugante as a secretary. Did you talk to Laura?"

"I'll give you a call later."

"Oh, that is so good of you. Did you–"

I eased the phone to the hook. I didn't mind calling the cops or even going up to Misty Crest Road with Sandiri, but I was not going to go up there alone and get myself accused of the murder. The cops would eventually talk to me and to Prendergast. If I told them now, they would figure out that I had been there and I would have some explaining to do.

Right now, I had to put some time in working for Trugante or I would be in a different kind of trouble.

* * * *

I drove home, parked my car on the lot behind my building and took the five-minute walk to the bar on Cahuenga Boulevard called the Yucca Café. It's an ugly name for a bar, a street, a flowering plant or anything else you cared to hook it to, but the place had good food, decent drinks and nice help.

Trevor, the good-looking blonde kid, was tending bar. There were too many people left over from lunch for him to relax much. The lunch crowd was devoid of the minor technicians and writers from the nearby studios, but some of the extras from Central Casting were scattered around the room drinking water or nursing beers. They were all looking for their big break. Today, they weren't even hired as extras.

I asked for plain soda and a ham sandwich.

A little brunette who reminded me of Judy Garland was sipping from a Coca-Cola glass hoping to be discovered. Fat chance. For the image she put up, she was better off at a soda fountain. She looked down the bar at me and grinned.

I smiled to myself. Maybe it was a different kind of discovery she was looking for.

Trevor brought me the soda. He waited on two other customers while someone made my sandwich in the back. When he returned, I asked if he remembered Alice Smith.

"Didn't you used to go with her?"

"Once or twice. I'm looking for some of her friends."

"She had some. Yeah. Everybody's got friends."

"I mean close friends."

"Like you were?"

"Yeah."

"You're on a case, right? I never saw you working on a case before."

I gave him a couple of names. He didn't remember them at first, but after a couple of walks up and down the bar while he waited on other customers they came back to him.

"Yeah, I remember them now. They thought they were going to be stars. They went back East, I think."

"Friends?"

"Not my friends. Not each other's friends either, I don't think."

"They fought?"

"I don't think they even knew each other – at least not very well. One guy was before you. The other guy was right after the bodybuilders."

The fact that they had left town was not enough to take them off Trugante's hook. I was sure that he had friends back east. I asked Trevor if he knew how to get in touch with them.

"Joey Hayes, I think one name was. I don't know about him. But Walter Cranbrook played football at UCLA. You could probably check him at the registrar's office."

"Big guys?"

"Not as tall as you. Pretty muscular."

I was barely six feet.

Trevor went away to wait on another customer and I bit into the sandwich, which was good. I decided that Trevor had never been involved with Alice, so it was okay to pump him. When he pulled my glass to refill the soda, I asked him if he had seen either of them with Alice lately.

"Off and on, I saw both of them. She was a good-looking girl, but she was always buying guys drinks. It was like she had to buy their company, like with you. She came in, looked around, and zing, she went straight to your table."

"I was only with her once or twice."

My face started to burn at the lie. I was trying to talk myself out of ever being with her. Not because the couple of weeks weren't fun, but because of the situation I was running up against. I didn't want to be the groom to a mob boss's daughter, and I damn sure didn't want to get murdered as a wedding present.

"What was the look for?" I said when he came back.

"You might've been with her once or twice, but..." He let the words trail off. Bartender or not, Trevor was not one to spread gossip, especially when the gossip was about the one he was talking to. "I don't know that you ever made a scene, but she sure did."

I thought back about it. He was right. The first time she came into the bar, she covered me like a downpour. Whenever we were together, she pulled my arm in as if she wanted me to protect her. When we sat at a table, she would move so close that people might think we were in love. As soon as we'd walk into my apartment, she was tearing off my clothes.

Even admitting it to myself is embarrassing. She was twenty now and only nineteen then. I was already in my thirties, and not long back from the war, and I was as horny as a stud bull.

"Anybody else ever come in with her?"

"The bodybuilders."

"Not the same as Joey Hayes and Walter Cranbrook?"

"No."

"How long did the bodybuilders hang around?"

"Month, maybe two."

"Anybody else? Anybody recently?"

"She hasn't been in."

"How about her last?"

"Tall guy, gray hair, good looking, maybe late forties. They fought some."

"Was he in the movies?"

"If he was, I never saw him. He was only in with her."

I had been hung up on Alice for a while, maybe even a little bit in love with her until after the bodybuilders. Eventually, I realized that it wasn't even love, just hurt pride. I missed the sex and I didn't like getting pushed aside for two guys who could have played apes in a jungle movie.

For no good reason, I switched from plain soda to soda with Scotch. I had only two, so I wasn't drunk, but I sure was thinking about my time with the little blonde who turned out to be the daughter of Salvatore Trugante. They were two draining weeks and I never did a dollar's worth of work during that time.

I finished my Scotch, left a dollar tip for the booze and the information, and I rose to leave.

"Wait a minute," Trevor said. "One more name. Merriman.
Norman, I think. Maybe Norman Merriman, Junior. I heard her call him
'Junior' once. I think he does the waves at Santa Monica."

I was in no mood to go on a wild surf chase. The lady I had been
looking for was dead, and if I had been quicker last night, I might have
prevented it. Maybe the second drink was one too many, because I was
feeling rotten.

* * * *

I went home for my car and drove back to the office. When I arrived,
the door was unlocked. I eased it open to see the back of Marco Sandiri's
head as he sat in the swivel chair that he had dragged all the way across
the office.

He was staring out the window at the Palladium. It was a habit I had
developed myself. There was something soothing about the empty
wooden squares over the marquee. When I looked out, I heard music in
my head. Sometimes it was Glenn Miller, although I had never seen him
there. At other times, it was Stan Kenton, who I had enjoyed, but had
trouble dancing to. On a day like today, I would be thinking slow music,
maybe even dirges.

"You been busy, huh?" Sandiri said without turning to face me.

"I'm always busy when I'm on a job. What do you need?" I closed
the door behind me, crossed my arms, and eased my behind to the edge
my desk.

He turned on the swivel chair and looked at me.

"Hollywood precinct got a call about a body on Misty Crest Road.
Desk sergeant said some guy called it in but didn't leave a name. That
wouldn't have been you would it?"

"Why do you think it was me?"

Sandiri just looked at me.

"Yeah, it was me. There was no phone in the house. When I went to
a pay phone, I tried to call you first."

"I was away from my desk. Hollywood called it down as soon as
they heard the word 'body.' It was right after I got your message."

"Good detective work."

"I would probably have figured it anyhow. I went up there. It's my
case now. So, do you want to explain what happened? How did you get
the right address?"

"I'd like to hold onto that one for a while."

"You can't. I gotta know."

When he knew that I had information, I usually didn't keep it from
him. "Laura Prendergast's girlfriend told me – Dixie Joy, the one who
learned how to type and take shorthand."

"Where's she working?"

"At Sal Trugante's up in Laurel Canyon."

He raised his eyebrows.

"As a secretary."

"Did you know the body up on Misty Crest?" he asked.

"I was hoping to find her alive."

"You tell Prendergast yet?"

"I wanted to tell you first, but I'd like to be the one who tells him," I said.

"I'll think about it. What did it look like to you?"

"I saw a body hanging like a sagging triangle so I got the hell out of there. I only got close enough to see who it was and to check her pulse. I wasn't in the mood for details." It was a hell of an admission, but it was the truth.

"Lucky you. I had to stay and study it. People in this town are getting sicker all the time. Like that guy the Marquis de Sade."

"I know. How you gonna keep 'em down on the farm after they've seen Pigalle?"

"Who do you think did it?"

"A little guy in a bowler hat."

"What?"

I repeated the whole story about Laura leaving the Roosevelt Hotel with some inventor.

"A new movie system, huh?"

"I hate it when movie people are involved," I said.

"Movie people *or* politicians," he said. "And since we got the wife of one of the richest men in L.A., I think we're gonna have a whole lot of both."

"Look, I'm working for Prendergast and I blew it. Let me break the news to him?"

"You got an hour. Then we get him to come down and identify the body."

"She still hanging?"

"What do you think we are, perverts? We took our pictures and we took her down. I'm going to have to question you a lot closer on this later, you know. Some of those footprints in the dust are going to be yours."

"Maybe, but people were marching back and forth through there. And don't forget the guy in the bowler hat. He might still be registered at the Roosevelt. Are the papers going to tie this to the Dahlia?" I asked.

"Papers won't even know about it, if I can help it."

"How do you think you're going to keep it out?"

"Rick, you got a way of making me spill all of the police department's secrets, but that don't mean everybody else can. If Prendergast doesn't want it in the press, it don't go – especially since somebody's sure to hook it up with the Dahlia."

"You don't think so, huh?"

"Maybe if they had cut her in half, but not this time. What we got here is a shadow crime."

He read my look.

"It's a crime that gets buried in the shadow of another one. This one's in the shadow of the Dahlia and I hope to keep it that way."

"So's the cab driver."

"But that cat's already out of the bag and I don't see a connection," he said.

He rolled my chair across the hard floor and shifted his knees under my desk. "Not a bad sit." He rose from the chair, stepped to the door, and took his hat off the clothes tree. He turned to me and showed me his index finger.

"One hour," he said.

CHAPTER X

The butler led me into the library. Three of its walls were covered with books. The fourth had a window overlooking the golf course. Prendergast sat behind mahogany desk the size of a pool table.

"Mister Prendergast, I ... they found the body of your wife. She was murdered."

His look was blank at first, then his face shriveled into something like a raisin. His did a slow burn until his cheeks were scarlet.

"You were supposed to find her alive!" He emphasized each syllable.

"And I tried to do that. I saw her last night on the street. She was running from something. I stopped her and talked to her. Then she ran away."

"Who was she running from?"

"I don't know," I said.

"What did you say to her?"

"That you wanted her back."

"That was an asinine thing to do. And how the fuck did you lose her?"

Most of us lost that word when we came back from the war. Prendergast wasn't even in the war, but his former company provided some of the best fighter planes in the Pacific. Maybe he had associated with too many flyboys, but to my recollection, flyers used that word far less than the men in the foxholes.

I explained the situation.

"You let a woman get away from you?"

"She ran away. I was in my car."

"Then why didn't you get out of your car?"

"I did."

"You still lost her! You dumb motherfucker."

I never used that one.

"How much money do I get back?" he asked.

"Money?" I said. "You're wife's been murdered, and you're thinking about money?"

"It's not the money I'm thinking about. It's punishment for your damn stupidity. You should have grabbed her!"

"An advance is an advance, and it's mine."

"You cheap son of a bitch," he said.

"Yeah, I am." My cheapness comes from not having enough green, but I wondered where his came from. "Do you have any idea of who might have been chasing her?"

"Not one," he said, and he glared. "And why the hell do you care now? You have your fucking money."

Did I care? I mean really care?

Yes, damn it, I did. I cared about almost anybody who got murdered. I particularly cared when it had to do with a case I was working and someone was running for her life. I was supposed to find her and save her. I was supposed to bring her back to her husband. I was not supposed to let her get killed.

"I do care," I said.

"Get out of my sight."

I didn't even turn away from the desk. "You seem as upset about this as you would if somebody had just run away with the new Cadillac I saw you driving."

"Get out or I'll have you arrested for trespassing."

"Why did you want her back? Why didn't you just let her go?"

"Do you think letting her go would have saved her?"

I didn't answer.

He picked up his phone, called somebody and told them to call the police for some kind of vermin that was in his living room.

"The cops don't act as exterminators," I said, but I did not need a silly arrest on my otherwise clean record. There was no telling what judge would try my case or what influence Prendergast could wield with him.

"I'm sorry I didn't bring her back alive," I said.

He closed his eyes, opened them and pointed to the door.

"Albert!" he shouted. His eyes were glazed eyes, but there were no tears.

The butler came in. He raised his chin and clenched his jaw. "Sir?"

"Make sure that Mister Page leaves the premises."

* * * *

I knew damned well that I would find who killed Laura, but for the moment I was chained to Salvatore Trugante and his daughter.

If I believed Alice, I might be choosing who would die. But I had the sense that if death came, it would be for more than just getting Alice pregnant. It might come if he fought too hard against marrying her, or it might come if he did not show the proper contrition. It might come for some other reason that I could not even imagine.

54

I have to walk the occasional moral tightrope, but I had confidence that I could reach the other side without selling my soul.

I would not find Joey Hayes and Walter Cranbrook easily because they were out of town. I couldn't find their names in the telephone directory either, but I called information. The Cranbrook phone was disconnected and there were two Joseph Hayes. One Hayes was disconnected also and the other's voice sounded like it belonged to a man in his sixties. Since Joey and Walter had gone back east, I decided I would worry about them only if I dead-ended the other leads.

Norman Merriman, Junior was not in the Santa Monica directory. Finding him without a phone number or an address would be like finding a ten-penny nail in a haystack, which was possible. I went to a place called Kroner's, on Back Street south of the pier. It was a place where a lot of wave rollers hung out.

The sun was just about to disappear into the Pacific when I ordered a Scotch straight up. In a few minutes, at least some of the new class of beach bums would be coming in with their surfboards.

"What's an old guy like you doing in a place like this?"

The woman behind the bar was mostly blonde with a little gray thrown in for character. She had a pretty face and a nice smile. She was maybe ten years older than I was, but I was probably older than most of her clientele.

She told me her name was Connie and we made small talk for a few minutes, but she accelerated the process. "Okay, what are you here for? You a cop?"

"Private. I'm looking for somebody."

She touched both temples and rolled her eyes back, mocking the psychics. We were getting a lot of them in Los Angeles. In fact, we were getting a lot of everything.

"My voices tell me you are looking for a blonde man on a surfboard," she said in an exaggerated, ominous voice.

"Good guess. Guy in his early twenties."

She chuckled. "You might not be in the wrong place. The older ones hang out farther down the beach in Venice."

They were the real bums, I thought. "I don't think this one's very old."

"He got a name?"

"Norman Merriman, maybe."

"Normie? He'd be an all right kid if he wasn't so pissed off all the time."

"What do you mean by that?"

"He's got a chip. I think he's got a gripe with his old man. First time he ever came in here, he had a paycheck made out from a company with the Merriman name. I think it was his last check from home."

"Do you have an address?"

"Check cleared. That's all I cared about. It was on a bank in Pasadena. Little Normie should be in here in a few minutes. Gets chilly out there after the sun goes down. Hell, this time of the year, it's chilly all the time."

"He's little?"

"Figure of speech. He's young."

Speaking of young, the first kid with a surfboard came in with a girl who must have been twelve. They sat at a table in the corner, and Connie brought them two 7-Ups from the tap.

"Not him," she said coming back to me. "If his father don't want him, why are you trying to find him?"

"Somebody else's father wants a few words with him," I said. The words came out before I thought about them, but it turned out to be a break.

"Little blonde?"

"Good guess."

"Don't know what they ever fell out about, but there was rocks and fire and screaming. Before you know it, he's still here and she's gone."

"How long ago was that?"

"Two, three weeks? A month maybe."

The place was starting to fill up with mermen and mermaids and Connie kept leaving me to tend to business. Finally, she came back and asked if I wanted a refill.

"Don't think so."

"Here he is now," she said.

I glanced toward the door. Norman Merriman, Jr. was tall, good-looking, tanned and muscular. The peroxide actually looked good on him. He had a broad grin with far too many teeth. He was wearing a white T-shirt and dungarees, which he must have put on after he came out of the water, because they were wet in patches. He propped his surfboard against the wall.

Connie went over to wait on him, but before she got there, he spotted me and started for the door. He took his surfboard with him, and he was on the street before I managed pull it out of his hands, bouncing it to the sidewalk.

"Hey, shit! You know how much that costs?"

"You in a hurry?"

"Whatever it is, I didn't do it."

"Ever think you'd become a daddy?"

"Aw, bullshit! Ain't no way she sent anybody to–"

"Normie?" A blonde a little older than me came up to us.

"Hey, look, I get this all the time," Normie said.

"Because you're a movie star?"

"What's this all about?" the blonde asked.

"None of your business, lady."

"Leave us alone," Normie said to blonde and she was frightened. "Go!" He pointed.

"So you already know that you're gonna be a daddy?"

"Says who?"

"Normie?" the woman called. She was backing away.

"I told you, 'go,'" he said to her.

"Alice Trugante says."

"I don't know anybody named... Oh, shit."

The other blonde was walking away sideways and going down Back Street. She was not exactly afraid of him or of me. It was something else.

"Alice don't want me. She's got dozens to hang it on."

I believed that, but I also believed I might have the real daddy by the arm.

"Look I slept with her lots of times, but when she decided to take on every guy in Santa Monica, that was the end of it. I was finished. I was finished with everything. Shit, I knew I should have gone back to school."

I just waited.

"Look. I wasn't in on that rape. She was free and easy with me and I'll be damned if I know how many other guys. But that night, I had nothing to do with it."

He was a kid who had been waiting for the second shoe for so long that he dropped it himself.

"Tell me about it."

"I wasn't there."

The blonde was out of sight now.

"How about what lead up to it. What happened?" I asked.

"She was drunk, a lot drunker than usual. I told her I was through with her and she started playing up to everybody. 'Anybody wanna screw?' she hollers out."

"Where was this?"

"Mowgli's, in Venice."

"Why don't we go to your place and talk about it?" There is nothing like letting a man gather his belongings before you lead him to his cell.

"I don't have a place."

"The blonde?"

"Yeah."

"Then let's go to her place."

"She'll kill me."

"I don't think so. I saw the look on her face."

"She probably didn't go home," he said.

"You have a key don't you?"

"I guess."

As we walked along the sidewalk, the gritty sand crunched and rolled under our feet. It sounded like one a guy doing a soft-shoe and another slapping his thighs.

"Who was the ring leader?" I asked him as we walked south.

"If I tell you I'll get my balls cut off."

"And if you don't, I'll cut them off."

He stopped in the middle of the sidewalk. "Look, please–"

"Move," I said.

He turned between two buildings and we walked out to the beach. He was barefoot and I was getting sand in my shoes. After we walked about a hundred yards, I was wary that he would take off and I would be like some Keystone Kop stuck in the sand, but he didn't run and we finally stopped at a beach-front cottage.

"It's not my place. I mean, I just–"

I pointed to the door.

"Okay," he said. He unlocked it. He stepped inside and I followed.

When he flicked on the light, he turned toward me and looked surprised. I was even more surprised, because the last thing I remembered for a while was a *buang* sound, then the floor coming up at me.

CHAPTER XI

I thought somebody was carrying me and I heard voices, but the voices didn't make sense. Two male voices, maybe three, and one female. They sounded as if they were coming down a long tunnel. I think they had just taken me out of a car and they were carrying me. Yes, that was the feel. And there was a *plank, plank, plank* of hollow sounds. All the sounds were loud as if they were inside my head. But for some reason, I couldn't open my eyes. Maybe I was dreaming? But it was not a nice dream.

"On three, now. You ready?"

Somebody was swinging me.

"One."

They were still doing it, and with each swing, I felt my head dangle and roll.

"Two."

I was being swung higher.

"Three!"

What the hell?

I heard grunts and I felt myself going upward and floating through the air. I started to grab, but there was nothing to grab onto. Then I was coming back down.

Oh, Shit!

My arms and legs were flailing and I was falling, but I had no idea what was up or where was down. Then I hit something. Water. I was going under, far under water. I got a mouthful. I choked and I gagged, but the splash and the wet had brought me back to my senses. I was under and I think I scraped bottom but I wasn't sure.

My immediate thought was to swim to the surface, but I had no idea which way the surface was. As I struggled, I realized that someone had thrown me into the water and they expected me to drown. I was not going to let them kill me. I found my way up. As soon as I broke the surface, I knew they had thrown me off the Santa Monica pier and they might be waiting for me if I went straight to the beach.

The water was sucking and flowing but waves were not breaking and I realized that I was between the pier and the jetty that ran parallel to the beach. The current took me out, danced me around and brought be back. In the faint moonlight, I saw the pilings of the pier coming at me and I maneuvered my way between them and almost all the way to the beach underneath the pier.

No, I wouldn't go to the beach. Not to where they were.

I grabbed onto one of the pilings, tearing my coat and catching my shoulder holster. I had no gun, but the holster saved my life because it caught onto the piling and I would not have to go up on the beach. I was still groggy, but I had enough sense to know that somebody had tried to kill me and they hadn't given up yet.

It took a few minutes for me to regain my breath. I shed my coat and my holster. I held onto the piling and I waited. I was ready to wait them out, but I heard voices coming from under the pier.

"Get a boat," one of them called.

"Where the fuck we gonna get a boat?"

"Lifeguard boat," one of them said.

I knew it would take them a while to get a boat. I heard their voices. I could not recognize them or their words, but I sensed that they were in panic. They thought they were done with me, but they were wrong. They were running under the pier. Their voices sounded hollow. They shone a light, but I was behind one of the pilings. I took off my shoes and pants.

When the light flashed away from me, I went under the water and I struggled to swim north through and away from the pier. I ducked under again and swam up the beach. At least I thought it was up the beach. They would be waiting for me to come through the pilings and under the pier, but I would not be there.

I swam under the water whenever I could and sometimes I scraped the sand. I was trying to stay low so they would not see me. From time to time, I heard their voices fading in the distance. The few lights from the pier were fading too.

A heavy undertow caught me and carried me outward again.

Thank God there was a faint moon, I thought. I thanked him even more that I knew how to swim and that he had brought me conscious in time.

I peeled out of my shirt and tie. There were swells, but not many waves, because I was inside the jetty. Once in a while, an undertow would catch me and take me out, but I was patient. I cleared the jetty to the north and I finally rode my outstretched body behind some breakers. When the last approached the beach, I swam like hell. I had to swim even harder to miss the next breaker and a possible broken back.

By the time I was a hundred yards from the pier, I heard no voices, I heard only surf. It was time to hit the beach, I thought. I rode a swell and I swam with it. It didn't break until it was almost to the sand, and it slapped me down. I skidded, scraping my chest and shoulder.

I listened for voices, but there were none. I knew where my car was, but they would too, and they were more likely to have the key, because I was in my underwear.

Excuse me, sir. I don't have any money. Can I get on the bus? Or was it a streetcar? How the hell would I know? I had only been on the subway once since the war and a bus twice. I had no idea what routes they took, or how much they cost now.

* * * *

I had no identification, no gun, no money and no pants. All I had was me and my underwear. The few people who saw me on the street avoided me. I was still wet and shivering when I was picked up by the Santa Monica police.

"Whoa, Mister."

I started to explain as quickly as I could, but one cop opened the back door of their patrol car, and the other pushed me inside.

"We got some guy here who claims somebody threw him off the pier." One cop said into a hand mike.

"And he lived, right?"

"Just barely. You're alive back there, right?"

"Yes, sir."

"Why'd he jump off the–"

"I didn't jump I–"

"He says he didn't jump."

"Bring him in. We'll put him in the drunk tank."

"Roger, out." It was old military lingo, but cops were using it now.

"How many drinks did you have?" asked the cop who had not been on the two way.

"None. Actually, one. Somebody hit me on the head with a frying pan."

"And you remember that?"

"I remember the sound. I remember the hit. You can feel the back of my head."

"Fighting with the old lady, huh?"

"I wasn't fighting. I just got clonked."

They pulled up in front of the station and pushed me inside.

"Drunk tank for him," the desk sergeant said.

"Wait a minute," I said. "I'm a private detective. Sergeant Sandiri in L.A. Homicide is a friend of mine. Let me call him."

"You think I care about the L.A. cops? This is Santa Monica, pal."

61

"I'm not drunk. Somebody tried to kill me. They threw me in the damn ocean."

"Did they tie you up? Gag you?"

"No, but they threw me in the water because they thought I was out for the night."

"And you weren't drunk?"

"No."

"What were you snooping about?"

"That's confidential."

"I'll bet it is. Hose him down and see if you got some old clothes he can use."

"Can I call Sandiri?" I asked.

"Makes sense, Sarge," one of the cops said.

"After he changes. I'm not having a guy in underwear hanging around my muster room. After he gets some clothes on him, let him make the call. Then sit him in interrogation."

At least it wasn't the drunk tank.

An hour later, Sandiri came into the room where they had put me. He brought me a pair of pants that were too wide and too short and a shirt that was way too big through the chest, but the desk sergeant told me I to leave the stuff they had loaned me.

"Couldn't pay for dinner, huh? And wouldn't wash the dishes?"

"Funny," I said, but if I were in his place, I'd probably be trying to hold back a laugh too.

On the way to my car, I told him what happened and why I thought they did it. "I might have found the other guy though."

"What other guy?"

"The one for the pregnancy."

He rocked his head to the side. "You know, when you start to work for a guy like Trugante, it's not a good idea to be too efficient."

"Go to hell. Trugante didn't do this."

"I'm not kidding. If you're too effective for a guy like him, he won't let you go."

"What do you mean?"

"Think about it."

I didn't think much. They either took my keys or my keys were in my pants, floating around somewhere near the Santa Monica pier. Merriman and his girlfriend must have taken my gun, but they left me the shoulder holster, which a shark probably had by now.

Sandiri watched for only a few seconds while I tried to hot-wire my own car, but he became impatient and did it himself. He was a lot faster than I'd be and he knew what he was doing.

"I hope you got a spare key at home?"

"I do."

"I'll follow and we'll talk at your place," he said.

It wasn't comfortable driving in bare feet. It hurt whenever I pushed the brake. It was worse with the clutch.

I had a good lock on my apartment door, but even a good lock gives with the right aluminum-card action. I managed to undo it just as Sandiri was about to take the card from me and show me how.

"You need a better lock," he said.

I changed into my army fatigue pants and a T-shirt, and put Sandiri's donation of clothing in a grocery sack. He got us a couple of Scotches, put them on the cocktail table, and he commandeered my favorite easy chair.

"If I'm not supposed to give Trugante the kid's name, what am I supposed to do?" I asked.

"I didn't say don't give him the name, just take your time about it. No matter how big a hurry he's in, he'll be reasonable. And if you already know who the kid is, you're more than half done."

"As long as the kid stays put."

"Up to you to track him down again and make sure that he does. You sure he knows why you're after him?"

I thought back. "Yeah, he does. Look, Trugante sounded like he was in a hell of a hurry when he talked to me last night."

"I told you, he's reasonable."

"He didn't seem reasonable when his thug stuck a gun in my back. He didn't seem reasonable pointing his nickel-plated automatic across the limousine at me."

Sandiri didn't respond immediately. "I know what he expects. He doesn't expect miracles. Not quite miracles anyhow. Don't tell him who it is yet. Track the kid down and bring him in yourself if that's what it takes. Just don't let anybody hit you in the head with a frying pan again."

"That's not funny. It still hurts." I put my hand on the lump at the back of my head, but it hurt as much in the front now.

I explained that Alice Trugante was of the opinion that her father wanted to kill the guy who had knocked her up, and I didn't want Trugante turning the job over to me. If I came up with the name too quickly, he might ask exactly that, Sandiri said. He knew a lot about the L.A. crime bosses.

"You don't think Trugante would kill the kid do you?" I asked.

"And leave his grandson without a father? Not unless this Merriman kid did a whole lot worse than get her pregnant."

"He tried to drown me in the Pacific Ocean."

"That might put him down as someone to deal with very carefully, but you said there were four people."

"Three guys and a woman." I thought about it for a minute. The woman could have been Merriman's blonde, but I didn't think that any of the three male voices belonged to Merriman.

Sandiri had hardly touched his Scotch. I was finished with mine, so I went in for another.

"Tell me some more about this guy in the bowler hat. Who told you about him?"

"I told you everything I know. He and Laura left with the cab driver they found dead behind my office."

"I checked with the Roosevelt Hotel. No conventions Saturday night, but there was a party in about half-a-dozen rooms. They got complaints. The party broke up just after you say the cabbie picked up this guy with a blonde that fits Laura Prendergast's description."

"No inventors?"

"Nope."

"How about the guy in the bowler?"

"Not a registered guest, but the desk clerk saw a guy come through the lobby who reminded him of Charlie Chaplin."

"Way I heard it, it was a bowler, not a derby," I said.

"What's the difference?" Sandiri asked. "They did say there were a lot of good looking women and some horny old men."

"Just *old* men?"

"Mostly old men, but not that many. I figure Cameron for the party."

"No shit, Dick Tracy," I said.

"*Touché*. Did you talk to Cameron yet?"

I shook my head. "How about you?"

"Not yet."

"I'm definitely going to do that tomorrow." I looked at my too-slow watch, but it wasn't there. Some hungry fish must have gotten excited by the luminous dial and swallowed it whole. It was time for a new watch anyway. I leaned away from the stiff back chair and looked into the living room at the chef's belly clock on the wall. It was three-thirty in the morning.

"Make it in the afternoon tomorrow," I said. "I gotta get some sleep."

"Me too." He got up to leave. "You still owe me dinner."

* * * *

Merriman and whoever had hit me the night before had taken my gun. The only other gun I had was my .45 automatic from my stint in the army. It was the same kind of gun that me and a couple thousand other guys managed to bring back when Uncle Sam let us go in late '45 and early last year. I didn't have it registered, but I wasn't going to walk around unarmed.

I was trying to figure that out how to conceal the .45 without a holster and wondering if I should take more aspirins, when Dixie called.

"I truly would not mind seeing you tonight," she said.

I didn't really have a schedule, but one thing I did know was that I wanted to talk to Merriman again. I also wanted to go back to Cameron.

"If I come over, it'll be late," I said.

"I don't mind. As a matter of fact, I would love it if you came over here about eleven o'clock." It was a very interesting time, and I loved the way she said "oh-vah" and "he-ah."

"Where should I come?"

"The Hollywood Vista, of course."

"Are you still afraid to go home?"

She didn't answer for a few seconds. Then she said, "I don't think I can do that. At least, not yet."

"Eleven at the Hollywood Vista then. Can you put me through to the boss?"

"Why would *I* want to do that?"

"I'm doing a job for him, remember?"

"All right, but would you do me the biggest favor and call back in a few minutes? I would rather him not know that you and I have been talking on a personal basis."

So there it was. Maybe it was smarter to stay away from her, but I'm not always smart.

* * * *

When Dixie answered the phone less than five minutes later, she was cryptic.

"Mister Trugante has been trying to get in touch with you," she said, acting very formal. "Yes, he is right here. Mister Trugante will take your call in his office."

I almost led off with the story about locating Merriman, but I caught myself.

"What d'ya got for me, Page?"

A bad lead for Trugante would be worse than no lead at all, and a good lead would have him expecting too much.

"Nothing solid, just a couple of things. Do you know a guy named Cameron?" I was playing stupid.

"Why you asking about him?"

"I need an introduction."

"To find the guy who screwed up with Alice?"

"Partly. Yes, sir."

"Are you working another case besides mine?"

"Not really," I said. Technically, I was doing nothing for Prendergast, but I had an emotional need to find Laura's killer. "I just want to learn some things."

"You want to explain what you mean by 'Not really?'"

"I had a case I stopped working on after I took yours."

I explained that I was no longer working on someone's missing wife and that led him into more questions than I cared to answer – or even could answer. By the time he got through with me, I felt like he had whipped with a switch. Every answer I gave led to another question. The one he kept coming around to was, "How does you talking to Cameron help me find who got Alice with child?"

He beat on that enough that I finally came up with the stopper. "I think whoever did it might be one of Cameron's customers."

"Customers?"

I explained Cameron's call-girl business as if I had just learned about it.

"You think some bastard who goes to whores knocked up my Alice?" he asked.

"I'm checking all the possibilities."

"I won't call him, but you can say that whatever he tells you is in *my* interest."

"Yes, sir. Thank you."

"How did you know I could have any influence on him?"

"You have influence on everyone," I said. I did not know how I came up with that one, but it worked because it seemed to make him happy.

I was sweating when I hung up. My headache was worse, but I had to fix things as quickly as possible.

* * * *

Even in January, it is not very cool in Los Angeles. Well, maybe cool sometimes, but rarely cold. I don't like wearing my army officer's trench coat unless it's one of those rare times when it's raining or threatening to rain. It makes me look too much like I'm playing the Sam Spade or Philip Marlowe role. Too many other guys in my business are doing that lately, but the two-way pocket of my trench coat was a good place to stash my .45 automatic.

It took me a few minutes to rewire my car so that I could use my spare key and drive back to Santa Monica. I may get clonked on the head every once in a while, but I've got the kind of memory that grabs onto the things that happen before somebody clonks me – like the location of a beach house.

Too many more frying pans though, and I was going to end up with my brains scrambled like Mickey Wren. When I thought of Mickey, I thought of the voices from last night. His was possible.

I parked my car on the street and walked around to the beach side. Without knocking, I tried the door of the cabin. It was unlocked and I pushed inside. I held back and looked behind the door in case somebody was hovering with a frying pan. From the sound, I was almost certain it had been a frying pan but I didn't actually see it, so it might have been a pot. The way I figured it, it was Merriman's blonde who had used it on me.

Because of the brightness that glowed from behind the venetian blinds, it wasn't dark in the living room or the kitchen. But even with the sun angling in on the backside of the building, the curtains over the blinds kept the bedroom dark.

I flicked the light switch.

There were no bedclothes – no sheet, no blanket and no pillowcases. I eased to the closet and opened it. No street clothes either. I took my penlight and shone it on the floor and up on the shelf.

Nothing.

And nothing in any of the drawers.

The cabinets in the kitchen had no food. Just utensils and some basics like salt and pepper. There were three pots of different sizes but no frying pan. The medicine cabinet in the bathroom was empty too. The place was clean.

When I closed the medicine cabinet, I saw a big, broad-shouldered guy in the mirror.

CHAPTER XII

The man who stood in the doorway wore a crewcut, a Hawaiian shirt and blue bathing trunks. I thought he had a small gun in his big hand, but it was a set of keys.

"Can I help you, pal?" His accent was thick. New York, but slower as if he had been living out here for a while.

"I'm looking for the people who–"

"They checked out this morning, early."

"Guy named Merriman?"

"Lady named Patty."

"Blonde?"

"Yeah, stacked. She rents just about every week. Same guy with her every week."

"How about the lady's last name?"

"Drake. You a cop?"

"Private."

"What d'ya want her for?"

"It's a long story."

"It always is. You can talk while I check the place out."

"For what?"

"Make sure you didn't take anything."

"There wasn't anything to take."

"We'll see."

He made the same rounds that I did, but when he looked into the cabinet under the kitchen sink, he stooped low and did a kind of double check.

"That explains it," he said.

"What?"

"I found a frying pan on the beach this morning. Why anybody dumps a perfectly good frying pan is beyond me. It's coming back in here as soon as I check you out."

While talking to him, I almost forgot about the pain in my head, but it was still there.

"Was it an iron frying pan?"

"What the hell do you care?" he asked.

"Another long story. When do you expect her back?"

"She calls ahead. Usually comes Monday through Friday morning. She checked out early this week."

"You saw her this morning?"

"No. She dropped the key through the slot. She left a note that said she'd call. It's no green out of my pocket. She paid up front for four days. Always does."

"I didn't know these things were rentals."

"Is that why you were snooping around? Wanna rental?"

"I'm looking for a bleached blonde kid named Norm Merriman."

"Didn't know his name, but I think he's mostly her boy."

"Mostly? Does she ever come with somebody else?"

"Boys like him and men like you."

I did not take that as a compliment.

"Same guy a month or two at a time. Blonde kid's been her regular the last few weeks. What's your name?" he asked.

I told him, and he dangled a set of keys in front of me. They had *R.P.* on their brass disk. "These yours?"

"Yeah."

"How come they were on the beach?"

"Beats me, but I'll take 'em."

* * * *

When I stepped into the lobby of the Tower on Sunset, the desk clerk gestured frantically to Mickey Wren.

"Please tell Mister Cameron I'm here on the business of Mister Salvatore Trugante," I said to the clerk. By that time, Mickey was stepping up behind me.

"What're you doing here?" Mickey clamped his hands on my shoulders.

"He's here from Mister Trugante," the clerk said.

Mickey released me immediately. The desk clerk called upstairs. I didn't hear what he said, but there seemed to be some convincing going on. I wasn't sure who was convincing who or about what.

Finally, the desk clerk sighed and turned to me. "He says you can go up. Ninth floor... Mister Cameron says it's okay," the clerk said, but it didn't seem to be okay with Mickey.

"I'm goin' with you," Mickey said.

"That's very polite of you."

He squinted. "I'm still goin' with you."

As we went up, I asked him if he worked for Cameron or the hotel.

"None of your beeswax."

69

"You must be a pretty good bodyguard."

"Mister Cameron says I'm one of the best."

The elevator went nonstop from the lobby. When it reached the ninth floor, Mickey made sure I got out first. As far as he was concerned, I had put one over on him when I got away without answering his questions on Monday. He wasn't going to let it happen again.

"That door there," he said gesturing to one of three in the octagonal space.

I started to grab the art-deco latch.

"Knock first!"

I knocked.

Michael Cameron, who I had never met, looked like the classic man of leisure with his red ascot and wine-colored smoking jacket. He even had a pipe in his hand. It was a Hollywood image that too many guys were doing and it was getting funnier all the time.

"What does Mister Trugante want of me?" he said in a most pretentious fashion.

He gestured to a huge velvet sofa with a curved back that reached halfway up to the twelve-foot ceiling. He had me sit in the middle of it like it was an oversized throne, but it was so soft that it just about gobbled me up.

"He just wants a bit of information," I said.

He sat in a high-back chair in the same style, but he sat taller.

"I'd like to run a few names by you," I said.

"Couldn't we have done that on the telephone?" He looked at Mickey. "Don't stand there like an idiot. Get us something to drink – what will you have, Page?"

"Scotch, a little bit of soda. No ice."

"Yes, sirs," Mickey said and he hurried to another room. I had never heard the word *sir* used in the plural before.

"What do these names have to do with?" Cameron asked.

"A couple of things. Do you know a woman by the name of Patty Drake?"

"Of course. She was a star at MGM."

"Star?"

"She was featured in several movies."

I nodded. I went to the movies every week or so, but I didn't remember seeing her on the screen.

"How about Laura Fane?"

"She worked for me too. What's this all about?"

"Just checking some things."

"Laura left because she married some millionaire," he said. "I'm quite proud of that."

"Did she work for your escort service?"

"In a peripheral way, yes."

"Dixie Joy?"

"What did you do? Find some of my old payroll records?"

I grinned. Yeah, like he kept payroll records.

"Yes, her too," he said. "Dixie learned how to type and take shorthand and now she's working as a secretary someplace." The "type and take shorthand" line was beginning to sound like some kind of pitch, but he damn well knew where Dixie worked.

"Do you ever hear from Laura Fane? Her name is Prendergast now."

"I saw her Saturday night coming out of the Roosevelt Hotel."

"Who with?"

"Not her husband. Are you working for Prendergast?"

"What time did you see her on Saturday?"

"About one. She was with a little fellow... You are working for her husband, aren't you?"

"What did he look like?"

"Nondescript, small, gray-haired, nice suit, bowler hat. I think it was a bowler hat. We were in the lobby and he was holding it in his hands."

"Do you know anything about a meeting of inventors?"

"Inventors?"

"I suppose that's what you'd call them. People who devise new techniques to make movies."

"No."

"Were you at a party at the Roosevelt?"

"I had dinner with friends."

"At one in the morning? In six rented rooms?"

"Where did you get all this information? I had dinner with friends. We were coming back for drinks at the Roosevelt. Are you sure Mister Trugante sent you?"

"I'm trying to do a job for him, so please bear with me. Do you know his daughter?"

"Not well, but I'd know her if I saw her on the street."

"She's a blonde now, you know."

He chuckled. "I'll bet Sal loves that."

"He didn't say. Do you know anyone who might be seeing Mister Trugante's daughter?"

I waited as Sal might if someone was trying to avoid an answer.

"She's seeing some cab driver," he said.

That one threw me. "That doesn't sound like somebody who—"

"Young women are stupid, Mister Page. The driver's name is Paul France. I think he drives for Wilshire."

"How about Norman Merriman, Junior?"

"How about the Duke of Windsor?"

"What does that mean?"

"It means that whoever this guy is, he's got a fairy name that's what it means, and I *don't* know him." Those were harsh words coming from a guy with an ascot.

"Do you know Merriman?"

"Like the sole of your foot."

"Sounds to me like you're trying to avoid answering the question."

"I have never heard of him." When he first started to talk, he had his nose in the air. Now he was leaning his head and shoulders closer to me with each answer.

"Okay. When's the last time you saw Alice?"

"Alice?"

"Alice Trugante."

"Oh, her. I saw her at a party for John Wayne over at the Republic Studio. She was hanging all over him. The Duke wasn't happy about it and neither was Herb Yates, but they didn't want to upset Sal, so they let her make a fool of herself."

"Sal was at a Republic party?"

"Because Alice wanted to sit on John Wayne's lap," he said and he smirked.

"When was that?"

"Middle of the war sometime."

"How old was she?"

"Sixteen or seventeen, I think."

"You think she ever saw Wayne again?"

"Hell, he got out of there at his first chance. If he saw her first, I'll bet he made sure that she didn't see him."

"How'd she take his leaving the party?"

"How? She took it out on her father, that's how. If she were a man, even a son instead of a daughter, I'd think you'd have to visit some graveyard to speak to her. You're not taking all this back to Trugante, are you?"

"Not all of it. Do you think she ever saw Wayne socially?"

"Hell, no. Sal was as embarrassed about the whole thing as Wayne was. He wouldn't stand for her making a fool of herself again. If you knew Sal..."

"He wouldn't stand up for his daughter? I thought that the Italians—"

"Don't demean the Italians, Mister Page. The Romans were the beginning of Western civilization."

"I thought it was the Greeks."

He didn't reply, and that was the extent of that argument.

My thought was that Alice would see Wayne just as freely in public as in private. Then it occurred to me that she had introduced herself to me as Alice Smith.

When I first met her, I took the idea that her name was Smith about as easily as I would have taken Jones or Brown. I had no idea that she was related to Trugante, but I was learning rapidly that a mob boss might wield as much power as the boss of a major studio. So far, Cameron was answering my questions without complaint.

"How would he ever know if his daughter was seeing John Wayne or anybody else?" I asked.

"I don't like you, Page."

"I didn't ask you to like me. I'm just asking a few questions. How would Sal ever know about it?"

"He has ways, Mister Page. Now if you will excuse me, I have several phone calls to make. My business does not run itself."

"I'll bet it doesn't," I said.

"I will be calling Sal to make sure that he sent you," he said.

"I thought you did that before you let me come upstairs."

His cheeks turned red. "Thank you, Mister Page... Mickey, will you show Mister Page to the lobby."

"Have you ever dated Alice?"

"Don't be impertinent," he said.

* * * *

Where there is a Norman Merriman, Junior, there's usually a Norman Merriman, Senior. I didn't remember seeing such a person in the L.A. or Santa Monica phone directories, so I went to the public library downtown and looked through those of the surrounding communities. I found a Norman Merriman in Pasadena, with separate home and office numbers.

The office was in a low, one-story plant that covered a quarter of an entire block on Colorado Boulevard. One entrance for Merriman Printing and Publishing had *For Solicitors* painted on the door glass, but I went through the other.

"My name's Richard Page, I'd like to speak to Mister Merriman."

The little redhead looked up at me through thick glasses. "Can I tell him the nature of your business?"

"I want to talk about Mister Merriman, Junior."

"Oh," she said. "Yes. Well... Oh."

She had an intercom on her desk, but she chose to go down a long corridor, tapped on a door and went inside. On her way back, she watched her feet in front of her. She did not look up until she was in the outer office again.

"He says, uh, that you should go on back. Third door on the left."

I tapped on the third door. A tall man, whose hair was a mix of dark and gray, reached out to shake my hand. His palm was clammy.

"Yes, sir. What can I do for you?"

"I'm trying to locate your son."

"Is he in some kind of trouble?"

"A minor kind of trouble."

"You aren't the police, are you?"

"No, sir."

"Then I'm afraid I don't have to deal with you. I'm a busy man."

"That sweet? That simple? Too busy to worry about your son?"

"You said 'minor trouble' and you're not a cop, so I'm afraid that's all you'll get. My son betrayed me and I'll have nothing more to do with him."

"'Betray' is a harsh word."

"Nonetheless, an appropriate word. And if you're fishing for an explanation, you've lost your bait."

"My bait?"

"I said, 'Good Day.' In case they don't understand that where you live, it means, 'get the hell out.'"

"Yes, sir." I knew he wouldn't take it if I handed it to him, so I placed one of my business cards on his desk and reached for the door.

"You can take that with you."

"That's okay. I've got plenty."

When I reached the outer office, the little secretary was fumbling with her purse. I could almost hear the foot tapping of the fiftyish woman who was waiting to take the receptionist's seat.

I was on the sidewalk. I had just fired up a Lucky when the little redhead stepped outside. She was not as interesting without her glasses.

"Oh!"

"You had lunch yet?" I asked.

"No, but I'm not having lunch with you." She hurried past me.

CHAPTER XIII

The secretary walked away from me, clicking her heels on the sidewalk and pretending speed, but she knew I was coming after her.

"Are you sure you don't want lunch?" I said when I caught up with her.

"I can buy my own lunch, thank you."

She turned the corner quickly with a twist of her ankle, and she started to topple. I grabbed her to keep her from falling, unintentionally touching her breast. Her face turned red, but she couldn't protest an act of gallantry.

"Sorry," I said.

"It's quite all right. Thank you. I would appreciate it greatly if you would stop following me."

"What's all the secrecy about?" I asked.

"I don't want Norm, Mister Merriman, to know." I had guessed right, but the "Norm" part surprised me. She kept walking and I stayed up with her.

"You know him well enough to call him 'Norm?'"

"No." She shook her head. "No."

"Hmmm."

"Get your mind out of the gutter," she said.

"Where are we going?"

"*We* are going no place. *I* am going home."

"So what do we know about young Mister Merriman?"

She stopped in the middle of the sidewalk. "Do you know where he is?"

"I was hoping you could tell me about him."

She raised her nose and started walking again. Finally, she stopped in the driveway of a large house. I waited for her to start talking. When she did, the words came out in a flood.

"Normie's a good boy, Mister Page. He was only in the army for six months. He didn't even go overseas. He flunked out of officer training and they just sent him home. Norm didn't like that and he didn't like it when Normie told him he wasn't going back to college. Norm wanted him to come to work at the plant. Normie didn't want to do that either, but he did it anyhow."

She paused for a breath.

"He didn't like starting at the bottom. He really, really didn't like that. But he came to work every day, every – single – day. In early, out late, hating every minute of it. Then Norm finds that Normie is seeing Patty and Norm doesn't like that, and–" There were tears in her eyes.

"Hold on. Who's Patty?"

"She's a woman in her thirties, but quite attractive. She talks him into going down the beach. He says, 'to hell with everything at the plant, to hell with the future, and to hell with you too, Dad!'" The redhead turned her head abruptly and looked straight at me, her lips pursed. She was doing everything she could to fight back her tears.

"Don't tell me Normie was screwing you too?"

Her mouth fell open. She shook here head. She raised her hand. "Yes."

"And Norm didn't like that?"

"I think you'd better leave." A little crying sound came out that time, but still no tears. We were still in her driveway. She took out a handkerchief and blotted her eyes. She sniffled and blew her nose.

"Where is he?" she asked.

"He was in Santa Monica last night. I don't know where he is now."

"Is he all right?"

"Yes, but don't get your hopes up. I think he's still wrapped up with her."

"Did he get someone pregnant?"

I guess there was some logic to that conclusion. "I'm not at liberty to say."

"Oh," she moaned, and she sniffled into her handkerchief.

I felt sorry for her, but there was hope. If she didn't find Normie, there was always Norm.

* * * *

I've only been a private eye since the end of the war and I'm still learning my way around. Before Monday, I had only a vague idea of who Michael Cameron was and what he did, and I didn't know about his connection with Salvatore Trugante. I wanted to know more about Patty Drake, so I got in touch with Sandiri in his office.

"I don't think she does calls anymore, she's in semi-retirement. She used to have a house. Before that, she did high-class calls. Never worked for Trugante as far as I know, but maybe Cameron. She still has special customers. What else do you need?"

"Was she missing for any period of time?"

"Missing?"

"Out of touch with everybody."

"Rick, I know *about* her. I don't know every move she makes – or made."

"Do you have an address?"

While he was looking it up, I was thinking about the luck. If Patty Drake was the woman who banged me over the head, finding her could solve a lot of my problems. It might all tied in. It wasn't coincidence or even fate. It was somebody's plan.

Sandiri came back and gave me an address in the hills over Sunset that was within a five-minute walk of the Tower.

"What do I do? Knock on the door and say Sgt. Sandiri sent me?"

"Better than saying Joe sent you."

"You're serious?"

"Yeah, I'm serious. Tell her you know me," he said. "Tell her this is strictly quiet stuff. She'll answer questions with no sex for twenty bucks a half-hour. If you want more it'll cost you more."

"Is she famous or something?"

"Not famous, just good. Well, maybe famous in some circles."

"You a customer?"

"Not in a while."

"This is a whole house, right? Lots of girls?"

"No. This is where she lives. She's retired – mostly retired. She's got a little heft, but it's all in the right places."

* * * *

Patty's place, like just about everything in the hills, was on a winding road. It was not a mansion, but nothing else on her street was either. I knocked and after a few seconds, the door opened. When she saw me, she tried to slam it, but not before I propped the door open with my leg.

"I'll call the cops," she said.

"Sandiri sent me."

"Who? Oh, What do you want?" She stopped fighting me over the door.

"I want to talk."

"I don't want to talk to you."

"Sandiri doesn't know about you slugging me." Lies always come in handy.

She was quiet for a moment. Then she pulled back the door.

"I'm sorry about the frying pan." She did not invite me to sit, but she let me inside.

Her furniture was reasonably new. The sofa and easy chairs were squared off with wooden legs. The cocktail table was kidney shaped with nothing on it. The impression of the room was white, bright and

77

tastefully modern. Her blonde hair was wavy. She seemed dressed for the evening although it wasn't five o'clock yet.

"I wouldn't have hit you, but I was afraid you were going to take him to his father."

"Would that be so bad?"

"His father wants him locked up."

"Stealing?"

"You're working for him, aren't you?"

"No, but there are only a couple of reasons a father would want to have a son locked up. Does it have something to do with you?"

"Why me?"

"Didn't you work for his father?"

"You sure do a lot of snooping."

"Yeah. Who helped you throw me off the pier?"

She squinted. "We didn't throw you off anything. We just dragged you onto the beach and got the hell out of there."

"You cleared out pretty quick. There was nothing in the apartment."

"We thought I killed you."

"You were clearing out while I was dead on the beach."

"Obviously, you weren't dead."

"You thought I was."

"It was an accident. And it was easy to clear out. When I go with Norm, I go light."

"Norm, the son, that is?"

Her cheeks went slightly pink. "There's only one Norm as far as I'm concerned. What's this business about the pier?"

"Somebody tossed me off it."

"Well it wasn't me. I took Norm home in a cab and–"

"Where's his home?"

She clammed up.

"I'm not trying to find him for his father and you know it. What can you tell me about Michael Cameron?"

She eased herself into one of the chairs and looked up at me, afraid.

"It's got nothing to do with Norm," I said. "It's for something else I'm working on."

"I don't know anything about Michael except what he does for a living."

"You used to work for him." Getting information out of her was like strangling a horse. "Let's not play stupid. I want to know everything you know about Cameron."

"Would you care for something to drink?"

"Just water. A little bit of ice if you have it."

She went into the kitchen. I saw her only at a glance last night and she looked pretty good. Sandiri was wrong. From my point of view, she had just the right amount of flesh everyplace. I had seen her before last night, but I wasn't sure where, the movies maybe.

The water was in a low-ball glass, maybe for effect. When she leveled those blue eyes at me, she reminded me of Dixie. I wondered if the eye-thing was MGM's training or just Cameron's.

She verified immediately that she had once been an MGM feature player, which meant that she had had a line or two in many of her pictures. MGM let her go before the mid-war purge. She thought it had to do with money, but she wasn't sure.

Cameron, she said, picked them up one by one. First her, then four of five other girls. With these additions, he expanded his escort service to include political and military big wigs. That was where she got started. The prices kept up with wartime inflation. She said that Cameron gave each girl a fair share of her take.

"I saved most of mine. And he got into some other business ventures. As far as he was concerned, I was done maybe a year ago. I already knew how to type and take shorthand."

There it was again, I thought as she continued to speak, "type and take shorthand." It was some kind of formula, every girl's dream of independence, even when you had been a hooker.

"Merriman knew me when I was still working for Michael," she said. "He sort of bought me from him. Paid for my independence so I could work full-time for him, but I didn't like the full-time work that Norm put on me. It was like working for Michael only worse. He was more demanding. He made me put in a full eight-hours in his office. I also had some very difficult nights and weekends with him."

"Was he into sadism?"

Her suddenly red face told the tale.

"Did he ever–"

"I'm not going to answer your ugly questions. I've told you too much already."

"Is that why you left Merriman?"

"Yes and no. I fell in love with Normie and we both got out of there."

"Do you own this house?"

"How do you get from me loving Norm to 'do you own this house?' Yes, I own this house."

"Who bought it for you?"

"Are you trying to be insulting?"

"Who?"

"I bought it for myself with the money I saved from the movies and from when I was with Michael."

"And not from the money Norm stole from his father?"

"No! What did Sandiri send you here to ask me? I'd like to get that cleared up so I can get you out of here."

I was beginning to feel that nobody wanted to talk to me. "He sent me because I'm working on a couple of cases that might tie in with the boy."

"What did he do?"

"Maybe nothing. If you thought you killed me, why did you leave the frying pan on the beach?"

"I've never killed anybody before and I didn't think about it. I must've panicked. No wonder we couldn't find it in the house."

"Who took my gun?"

"Your gun? Oh. Normie said you had a gun. He said we shouldn't touch it."

"So you left it with me."

"We dragged you jut far enough away so the lights from the cabins wouldn't advertise that you were dead."

"Thank you. Did you see anybody else you knew last night? Like Cameron or anybody that you know who works for him?"

"Why him? Why anybody who works for him?"

I described and named several people. She knew all of them, but nothing she said incriminated them.

"Do you know Alice Trugante?"

"No, but Normie does. Why do you ask?"

"Didn't Normie tell you?"

"No."

"Does Norm know her?"

"I don't think so, no." She looked at her watch. "Mister Page, I've answered all of your questions. Please ask me whatever else you need to know so I can get out of here."

My replacement watch showed four-fifty. I wanted to repeat several questions. All that would do was make me seem like a bully, and she was not likely to change her answers.

"Where's Normie?"

"Staying with one of his beach buddies."

"Where?"

"I don't think I will tell you that, Mister Page," she said. Then she insisted that I leave.

I opened my wallet and handed her a twenty-dollar bill. Her face went stern for a moment. Then she snapped it away from me.

* * * *

I went back to my office and called for messages. My only calls were from Prendergast and a "Mister Hastings." He might be a potential client, so I called him immediately. His line was busy and I figured he was fishing the Yellow Pages for a private detective. Prendergast, the cheap and uncaring bastard, probably wanted his money back, so he could wait.

I wrote checks for electric and rent, and I called Hastings again. The phone rang six times. I was about to hang up when somebody grumbled into my ear.

"Yeah?"

"Mister Hastings?"

"That's me." It was a hollow sound, like it was a phone booth.

"This is Rick Page, Rick Page Investigations. You called?"

"Keep your nose clean."

"Of what?"

"Of everything. Otherwise you'll get yourself et by the sharks for real." He hung up.

If he hadn't told me about the sharks, I wouldn't have connected him with the Santa Monica pier. He was one of the people who tossed me in. I thought I recognized the voice, but I couldn't be sure until I heard it again.

CHAPTER XIV

Young Merriman was still my number one daddy suspect. I went back to the Yucca Café to talk to Trevor. I would pass on dinner, but one Scotch would be just fine. A rush of studio people came in. He had to wait on them and send food orders back to the kitchen. The new crowd was the second-tier studio technicians, line writers, some bit players and extras. Hollywood was full of blondes, blondes and more blondes, male and female. It would be the perfect place for Cameron to do his recruiting.

When Trevor came back and asked if I wanted another Scotch, I told him no, but I asked how long he had working been here.

"Since I mustered out."

"You ever hear of a guy named Michael Cameron?"

"I don't think so. No."

"You said something about an older guy with gray hair you saw with her?"

"Once or twice. Is he Cameron?"

"I'm asking you that."

"Don't remember his name."

I tried a detailed description, but Trevor kept shaking his head. "To tell you the truth, he was more like her father than a boy friend. He was with her, but I never saw them leave together."

"Did he look anything like Merriman?"

"Merriman? No. Maybe a little. I mean this guy had gray hair though, you know dark and gray mixed. But they weren't together that much.

"Who worked here during the war?"

"Miss Kathryn. She owns the place."

"She ever come in?"

"Early in the morning. She opens up. Makes sure everything's good for the day."

"What time is that?"

"Four o'clock, way before the birds get up. Some of these people come in for breakfast on their way down to the Gulch. Some meet their rides up to Universal or over to MGM. Good bus connections down the block too."

I wondered how movie people managed to stay up so late and get to work so early. But I was probably thinking about the exceptions to the rule, the low-life stars that caused scandal and managed to keep the gossip birds chortling out front-page stories.

I thought about that some more while I was waiting for Trevor to come back. I thought about all the women and men who played goody-goodies on the screen, yet managed to get themselves into a jam with the press and the studios. Just as in the movies, everything was a façade. You hardly ever heard anything bad about the big stars unless someone died in the process. To hear Sandiri tell it, you sometimes didn't hear it then.

"What time do you open for breakfast?"

"Four-thirty."

It was too early to get up, but I would make the effort to come in and talk to Miss Kathryn.

Being knocked out last night was not very restful, and while I was listening to the gun dealer telling me about a holster for my automatic, I almost zinged off to sleep. If I was going to see Dixie at eleven tonight and be at the Yucca cafe at four in the morning, I had better get some sleep ahead of time.

I was back at my apartment and ready to slide between the sheets when Ty Prendergast called.

"If you'll accept my apology, I would like to hire to you again."

"For what?"

"I don't think anger on your part is called for, but even at that, I would like to talk to you if you don't mind."

"I am very sorry about your wife, but I don't have time for wild goose chases."

"You are still being belligerent, Mister Page. Will it help if I say 'I'm sorry' in those exact words?"

I thought about it. I didn't like Prendergast much and I'd be damned if I would apologize back. "I accept your apology, but if I am going to come all the way out Benedict Canyon. I want a full day's pay."

"For a man of my means, that is not much of an investment."

"Make it two days then."

"Come as soon as you can."

I needed the sleep, but money is an addiction. When I needed it, I needed it bad. When I didn't need it, I wanted more of it. I could talk to Prendergast and still get to the Hollywood Vista Motel by eleven o'clock.

"I'll be there in an hour."

* * * *

The butler led me into the library. Prendergast gestured me to one of the leather easy chairs and sat in the other. I must have been back in his good graces because he offered me a Cuban cigar, which I declined. He didn't take one for himself either.

"It has been one entire day, Mister Page, and the only thing the Los Angeles police department has done is to give me a call, apologize about Laura's death, and ask me to look at her body. I sent Albert."

Still sensitive aren't you, you bastard? "I'm sure that when they do come, they're going to ask you questions that will make you angry," I said.

He raised his eyebrows.

"In the death of a spouse, the survivor is always the first suspect."

"Even in a brutal case like this?"

"Especially in a brutal case like this." I thought of Laura, just the victim of a shadow crime that was eclipsed by the murder of the Black Dahlia. Somebody had to pay for that, and If they did it, I didn't care who it was.

"Are you trying to insult me?"

"I'm telling you how the police usually think. The longer they stay away from you, the better off you are."

"Should I get a lawyer?"

What the hell was I doing, helping a man evade a murder charge? "I'm sure you already have a lawyer."

"I would not have called you if I killed my wife. I want you to learn who killed her and turn that information over to the police since they seem too be busy elsewhere."

"Do you want the same kind of press for your wife's murder?"

"Of course not – but I have to know." He seemed sincere, but bastards like him are better liars than I am.

"It's not like in the books and on the radio, Mister Prendergast. Private eyes, old ladies and little Belgians do not solve crimes. The police do that."

"Nobody but the police?"

"Rarely anybody but the police."

"I am asking you to make an effort. The money of mine that you confis– The money I paid you to find my wife is fully earned. I will pay you another week's advance."

"Why not let the police do it? What's in it for you?"

"The satisfaction that my wife will be avenged and that somebody will care. And Mister Page, in spite of your rudeness, you give the distinct impression that you *do* care."

84

When I was here yesterday, he seemed to be more interested in the money than he was in his wife's death. Today it was different. I wanted to know why, and the fact that the police hadn't come to him yet was a good enough reason.

The rich could buy anything including justice – or the appearance of justice. I was not quite sure what Prendergast was trying to buy from me.

* * * *

A cute uniformed maid let me out of the place, and the front gate did its magical opening routine. I turned south on Benedict Canyon. In my rear view mirror, I saw headlights go on in a car that was parked about thirty yards behind the entrance.

I didn't wait to see if the car would follow, but I knew damn well that it would. I shifted through the gears rapidly and pushed hard on the accelerator.

With the other car behind me, I pushed to get up to a speed that would keep me well ahead of it. I tapped my brakes going into the curves and accelerated coming out of them. On the few nearly straight parts of the road, I saw the car coming hard behind me. I didn't think it was gaining on me, but I wasn't going to take the chance.

I didn't really know the drives and avenues but as soon as I knew I was in Beverly Hills, I hit my brake and slowed to about ten miles an hour. The other car was coming hard behind me. Still moving, I geared down, turned off my engine and lights, shifted into neutral and swung onto the first street to my right. My Ford tilted and almost went over, but it came down hard on its springs, bounced and slowed on an up-tilt of the slope.

I drifted to a stop, pulled the emergency brake and hoped they hadn't seen me make the turn. I turned on my engine, but not my lights, and I waited. It seemed easy, but they had made the mistake of turning on their headlights too early. The luminous dial of my new watch indicated ten forty-five.

Dixie would have to wait.

I opened my window and listened for other cars. I heard someone start an engine at a house ahead of me. Instead of waiting, I turned on my own lights, and moved past the driveway before the other car was on the street.

I felt safe with them behind me, but I had no idea where I was. I pulled to the side, let them pass, and started to follow. When we came to a wider road, I followed left, taking a calculated guess based on the glow against the haze that I would be headed toward Los Angeles and not away.

At the bottom of a long hill, the car stopped and turned right. I looked at the sign reading Sunset Boulevard and turned left toward West Hollywood.

I drove carefully, constantly shifting my eyes from the road in front of me to the rear-view mirror. At the same time, I was glancing into every side street and driveway to see if someone would start following me again. My chest was still heaving as I parked my car around the corner from the Hollywood Vista Motel, sat for a moment, then got out. I hadn't moved ten yards when a mountain stepped in front of me.

"You don't do like you're supposed to do," the mountain said. It was Mickey Wren. He was the one who made that anonymous call, and now I was sure he was one of those who tossed me off the Santa Monica Pier.

My gun and my new holster were under the seat of my car, and it looked like I was going to have to duke it out with Mickey.

I was not looking forward to it.

CHAPTER XV

"How you doin', Mickey?"

"How'd you know who I am?"

"I saw you stay in with Two-Ton Tony before the war."

"Didn't you already tell me that?"

"Not that I remember."

"I thought it was you."

"A lot of people saw that fight," I said. I tried to go around him, but he grabbed me by the arm and swung me back.

"Mister Cameron don't want you snooping in his business."

"What business is that?"

Someone spoke from the shadows to my left. "Any business he's got, smart guy." I did not recognize the voice.

"Yeah," said another voice. This guy stepped from behind a beer truck that somebody must have parked for the night, but it seemed like a stupid place to put it.

They had me on three sides.

"The swim didn't prove anything to you?" the one from behind the beer truck said.

"Proved I need to practice my back stroke."

"Or that you need to stay in the water a lot longer," said the one on my left.

The one from behind the beer truck sucker punched me in the jaw, throwing me all the way to the one on my left, who caught me with a fist to my belly and doubled me over. It was too good for Mickey to pass up, because he came with an uppercut that cracked my teeth together.

When my head went back, I swear I heard the *buang* sound of the frying pan again. I went dizzy but not blank. I came around with my right elbow and hit the one who had come from behind the beer truck and I kicked the legs out from under the one on my left. Mickey came lumbering at me with his hands down the way he must have come at Joe Louis, and I hit him with a hard right to the chin. It stunned him, but not like a punch from Louis. I hit him with a left too, which seemed to bring him out of the daze, and he brought his fists up in a boxer's defensive posture.

The guy on my left came up on his knees. He hit me with a weak left in the crotch, but I doubled over anyhow, and while I was in that position, Mickey hit me with another knee. He came up with a right under my chin again, and I went back onto the sidewalk. I didn't loose consciousness and I tried to turn over and go to my hands and knees.

"Not the head," the guy who had been on the left said.

After a fraction of a second, I felt a hard kick at my stomach and let out a heavy grunt. My hands went out from under me, and I went flat on my face.

"You gettin' the picture now?" one guy said.

I didn't have enough presence of mind to answer, and Mickey yanked me from the ground.

"You gettin' it?" said one of the other guys.

"You getting' it?" said the other.

"You listenin' Mister Page?" Mickey held my lapels, and banged the back of my head against the beer truck.

"Stop that!" a man called from the second deck of the motel.

"Mind your own business," Mickey yelled back.

"I called the cops," the guy up there said.

Mickey kneed me in the groin again. Somebody cracked me across the jaw. Then somebody, it had to be Mickey, picked me up, turned me sideways, and threw me against a palm tree. I hit stomach-first, wrapped around it, and slid all the way to the ground.

"If you don't get the picture, we kill you next time. You got it?" I had no idea who said that.

I was lying at the base of the palm tree, and I heard somebody starting a car.

"He's got it," one of them said, but it wasn't Mickey, because he was already climbing into the front passenger seat.

"Don't forget," the other guy said, and he climbed into the back seat. Somebody else was driving and it was none of the three, but I could not see who it was.

I was knocked out last night and I was dazed tonight. I had almost lost last night's headache, and now I had a new one.

I was curled around the palm tree and it seemed a good place to get some sleep. As I tried to figure out how they had picked up my trail, I straightened out and put my hands under my head. I thought about what happened tonight. About Prendergast and Mickey and about the two guys that I somehow thought were LAPD street cops in plain clothes.

None of it made any sense, but it was too complicated to think about.

* * * *

"Can you stand up?"

I opened my eyes and the light from the motel sign was shining straight into her face. "Are you an angel?"

"It's me, Dixie. What happened?"

"A mountain."

"What *are* you talkin' about?"

"Actually a giant." I remembered Mickey Wren and two other guys, and something made me think "cops."

"You are terribly messed up. Come on, let's see if we can get you to stand on your own."

"Did I ever tell you I like your accent?"

"You are so out of it, and so full of it."

"Out of what?"

"Out of this world."

"And full of – oh."

I used one hand to push myself up from the ground, and I leaned with my back against the palm tree. "I'll get it in a minute."

"Let's get you movin'."

"How did you know I was out here?"

"They were makin' enough noise to wake Mister Rudolph Valentino," she said.

She confused me, because Valentino had been dead for twenty years. I saw a flashing light and a car came to a stop in the middle of the street. Dixie helped me and I leaned my back against the palm tree. An LAPD cop in uniform came toward us.

"What's going on here?" It sounded like one of the same guys, but he couldn't get into his uniform that quickly.

"Some people were beating on him, officer," someone shouted down from the deck of the motel.

The cop looked up. "Thanks," he said and he asked me if I knew who they were?

"No, sir," I said.

"Did they take anything?"

"Not that I know."

"What was the beef?"

"I don't know that either."

"They just jumped him," the guy on the second deck said, with the enthusiasm of a man who must be a tourist – either that or he was new in town.

"You need an ambulance?" the cop asked.

"I *will* take care of him, officer," Dixie said.

"You his wife?"

"Yes, sir," she said. It was the easiest acceptable explanation, especially since she was in her robe.

I almost fell with my first step, but Dixie steadied me, led me along the sidewalk, then across the motel parking lot to the stairs.

"Thank you very much," she called back to the cop.

His light was still flashing and he stood there with his hands on his hips, probably considering whether to question me further, but Dixie kept me walking. I thought about Mickey and his two thugs and about minding my own business.

"Hold onto that railing," Dixie said as she helped me up the steps.

I was okay. If I had another concussion, it wasn't a bad one. I wasn't knocked out, but the blow made it easier for me to get some useless sleep. It was knockout sleep, not good sleep. It was headache sleep. I remembered being nestled around the palm tree and I chuckled.

"What ever are you laughin' at?"

"I was just thinking."

"Thinkin' what?"

"About a million things," I said, but I couldn't remember which were funny.

When she got me into the room, she sat me on the bed and took off my shoes. It was the kind of thing you would do with a drunk and I was groggy enough for that. Yeah. It wasn't a bad one, but I was knocked out again, wasn't I? Almost, anyhow. That didn't happen to me often and now twice in two days. Cameron was making it clear that he didn't want me asking questions no matter what Trugante had to say. I wondered which were the wrong things to ask, or was it everything?

I closed my eyes. Yeah, I did need sleep. I got up too early this morning after that thing last night, but last night they had tried to kill me. Today they had just beaten me. I wondered if it was different people, but they had to be the same. Same voices, I thought, but I wasn't positive of that.

"Your face is puffed up like a balloon," she said. I also had a new bump on my head. I think it was from the beer truck.

"Last night," I said, talking about the bump.

"Yes, and they beat the bejesus out of you." She thought I was talking about a few minutes ago, but I was talking about last night when – one, two, three – they tossed me through the air and off the end of the Santa Monica pier.

She wiped my face with a soapy washcloth and it stung a little. Then she came back with cotton and alcohol and it stung a lot.

"Ouch!"

"Sissy," she said, but she kept dabbing the alcohol and smiling through my pain.

After a while, it was just cool. The smell was soothing, and it acted like ether. She was doing a good job of taking care of me. The smell of rubbing alcohol was the last thing I remembered for a while.

* * * *

When I awoke, came to, or whatever-the-hell it was, I was in bed and somebody had her arms around me. Her bare breasts pressed against my back. My face hurt, my head hurt, my body hurt, everything hurt. I had recognized Mickey Wren, and only vaguely, the other two. L.A. cops. Somehow that seemed accurate, but it wasn't right that cops would be attacking me.

"What do you know about Cameron?" I mumbled, but Dixie had the slow steady breathing of someone who was asleep.

I tried to get back to sleep, but it wouldn't come. All I had was a headache and thoughts about my trip from Prendergast's estate. I wondered how they knew I was there, or if they had they followed me there in the first place.

It had to be the same people. Mickey was with them both times and last night, there was a woman. What went through my mind when I left Prendergast's estate was that they would try to drive me off the road. That might have killed me, but they probably didn't care one way or another. They just wanted me to stop whatever I was doing that affected them and I wasn't sure what that was.

If they were trying to cover up a murder, why didn't they just kill me outside the gate? I tried to think if anyone had said anything about a last warning, but tossing me off the pier should have been warning enough.

To hell with it, I wanted some sleep. I needed some sleep.

I awoke suddenly, jumped out of bed, and crossed to the dresser where Dixie had laid out everything from my pockets. For just a moment, I panicked, thinking that they had taken my .45, but I remembered that I left it under the seat of my car. I grabbed my watch. It was not dark enough to read the luminous dial. I carried it into the bathroom and the only light that was on. I opened the door all the way. The glare blinded me, but I was able to see that it was almost five o'clock and I was sure it was a.m.

"Very nice. Very, very nice," Dixie said as I crossed the room toward the chair where she had folded my pants and underwear.

"I have to get moving."

"Aw, are you goin' to leave me?"

She was sitting up in bed and even in the shadows, I saw how interesting her body was.

"You don't have to go so early, do you?" she asked.

I thought about the Yucca Café opening at four-thirty, and about Trevor telling me that Miss Kathryn came in at four, but that she didn't

91

stay very long. I would probably miss her anyway. Tomorrow would be soon enough.

"You are getting more interestin' all the time," Dixie said.

And I was more interested. To hell with the Yucca cafe.

I climbed on the bed with Dixie, put my arms around her, and lowered her to the sheets. Nearly every bone, muscle and organ in my body ached, but I had other needs. Dixie pulled the sheet from between us and lengthened her body under mine. She pecked me lightly on the lips, then again. She raked her fingers down my spine and touched the cheek of my ass, tickling me.

My back hurt. My belly hurt. My head hurt. I was amazed that I could feel anything as soft as a tickle.

She pressed her mouth on mine softly. It was partially open now. The tip of her tongue touching.

"They say that water seeks its own level," she said.

I had no idea what that meant, but that was just fine. She put one leg over my back, and her breast slopped to the side, but that was fine too. She moved her other leg, and I slid into a natural position.

"Mmm," she said.

"Yeah," I said. My back was killing me, but damn, yes. There were offsetting benefits.

"Yesss," she said.

Now I knew what she meant about water seeking its own level. We worked together, slow and interesting, with smiles and pecks and kisses. I was no longer thinking about the pain or about any case I might have. I sought only pleasure and I found it. The pain had gone, at least for a while, and I was in the arms of a beautiful woman.

When I awoke, it was already nine-thirty by my watch, and Dixie was not in the room. I remembered that she worked for Trugante and she probably needed to be there at eight or nine.

I had not asked her for all of the answers I needed, but I was sure I would see her again. She left a note saying that she was registered here for a week, that she didn't have maid service, but that I was not to worry about making the bed.

I had missed seeing Miss Kathryn at the Yucca cafe, but I could do that tomorrow. Obviously, I had needed the sleep.

I wasn't positive that they were Cameron's thugs. They could easily be Prendergast's thugs. Worst of all, they might be Trugante's thugs, so I would have to think before ratting anyone out to him. Two of them were L.A. street cops. I thought I understood how that could be, but I would have to ask Sandiri about that one.

CHAPTER XVI

I folded the paper, locked up the office and drove to downtown L.A. to speak to Sandiri. The Black Dahlia murder was still news, but there was nothing in the papers about Laura Prendergast. The homicide cops were doing a good job of keeping Laura's murder in the shadows.

It was eleven a.m. and the squad room was empty except for Sandiri and the lieutenant back in his glass cage. I was going to ask him about the Dahlia first, but he didn't give me a chance.

"What the hell happened to you?" he asked when I sat across the desk from him.

"Ran into a mountain."

"With your car?"

"With my face."

"You're walking like an old man. Something's going on Rick. They toss you off the pier one night and the next night they beat the crap out of you. Somebody doesn't like you very much."

I hadn't noticed the way I was walking, but I knew about the bruises. "Took a couple of your guys to do it."

"My guys?"

"Hollywood cops."

"Rubber hose treatment?"

"Somebody jumped me and gave me the big-fist treatment."

"You say they were cops?"

"Beat cops in civvies." I told him about somebody following me last night and jumping me in front of the Hollywood Vista Motel.

"What were you doing at the motel?"

"Tying up some loose ends."

"Sounds like somebody doesn't want you working the Laura Prendergast case."

"That's what they said, but why wouldn't the Hollywood squad want some help?"

"There's cops and there's cops." Sandiri looked at his watch and glanced over his shoulder at the lieutenant in his cage. "I need some lunch," Sandiri said.

He suggested an eatery we could walk to that specialized in barbecue. We were about a half-block from City Hall when he asked about the cops who beat me up. When I gave him the blow-by-blow, he said something I never thought he would never say.

"I think you gotta give up this case. It's like nothing you ever worked. You say street cops? You got names?"

"Had to be from Hollywood, but they were probably beating me up on their own time."

"All the more reason to drop the case. It means they're working for somebody with power. There's more money involved in this thing than there's gold at Fort Knox. It's why you gotta get out. Stop even thinking about this case. You got your hands full with the other one anyhow."

"Sandy..." I rarely called him that and I just let his name hang there. I shook my head while we kept walking.

"I'm not getting any of the money," he said.

"Neither am I, but this is the first time that–"

"There's a first time for everything. I told you we were going to keep it in the shadow."

"Because of the Dahlia?"

"Whoa!" He put up his hand and glanced over his shoulder.

"You told me they weren't connected," I said.

"I said that *they* said they weren't connected."

"Who's they?"

He didn't respond, but I should have known. The face and body of Elizabeth Short, the Black Dahlia, had been severely beaten, bruised, and her body cut in half. When they dumped her on a vacant lot, they had spread her legs. There were rope burns on her wrists and ankles.

Except for the murder, no one would ever have heard of Elizabeth Short. Now, she would live on in legend, while Laura Prendergast faded into oblivion.

For all of her dirty background, Laura was the wife of a millionaire when I found her hanging from that hook. I didn't stay around for the details, but I was sure there were rope burns on her wrists and ankles and that she had been beaten. From the way she was hanging, cutting her in half might have been the next step in the killer's process. Or maybe the cut-in-half thing was a special message with Elizabeth Short.

Sandiri never answered my question about who said the murders were not connected, so I asked him another.

"And what do you think about the connection?"

Again, he didn't answer. By that time, we were already heading into the restaurant on Fifth Street. We took a booth in the back.

"Did the same person – or persons–"

"We can't talk about this anymore," he said.

I nodded. It was a maniac who killed the Dahlia and a maniac who killed Laura. Maybe it was more than one maniac.

"You've been too sheltered, Rick."

"What do you mean sheltered?"

"You haven't been in L.A. long enough. The war took away years when you would have seen stuff."

"I saw stuff in Europe, believe me."

"Not the same."

He was betting that it was, but Sandiri had never been in the army. "Maniacs did both murders," I said.

"It don't take a psychologist to know that, but you and me, we're off the subject of the Dahlia... Did you read that Branch Rickey is bringing up some Negro kid from Montreal?"

"Never heard about a Negro kid playing for Montreal."

"Name's Robinson. Played football at UCLA."

Baseball was one of the few subjects that could take my mind off a case. I had never heard of a Negro kid playing at UCLA either, and I had my doubts that the Dodgers would get away with bringing him into a white man's league. My feeling is, if a guy can do the job, let him do it, but there were too many white Americans who still looked down their noses at Negroes.

It was too bad they weren't going to let Sandiri do his job, but that was for a different reason. He could tell me to lay off, but that was all he could do.

We talked Brooklyn Dodger baseball through lunch and back to City Hall. When I left him at my car, I asked him if the police had found the owner of the house that overlooked the Hollywood Bowl.

"I told you to lay off."

"You might lay off, but I won't."

He opened his mouth to protest, but he didn't speak. He just shook his head and walked away.

* * * *

I called Trugante and Dixie answered the phone. "You shouldn't be calling me here," she said.

"I wasn't calling you. I need to talk to Mister Trugante."

"Oh. Sorry. Hold on."

Trugante picked up the other phone and I heard him tell Dixie that he didn't need her.

"Yes, sir," she said. I heard her voice like it was an echo.

95

"What did you find out?" he asked me.

"People keep stopping me. I think they're working for Cameron."

"Not possible, not if you told him I said to cooperate."

"You know an ex-pug by the name of Mickey Wren?"

"Mickey, yeah. I made a lot of money betting against him when *Ring* magazine said he was the greatest thing since Dempsey."

I explained that I thought Mickey was involved in both of my beating incidents, but he let it go by. "So last night, what did you find out?" he asked me.

"Not much. I ended up with bumps, cuts and bruises, and I'm having trouble walking."

"You're trouble walking ain't my problem. My daughter's my problem and she better be your problem. What did you find out?"

I had my suspected daddy but based on Sandiri's advice I wasn't going to give him up yet. "I still have to do some checking. The names you gave me went back east, but I don't think it's one of them. Too long ago. I'm tracking some others, but I need cooperation. At least I need somebody to stop people from jumping me."

"You getting your licks in?"

"Some."

"Good. Keep on it. I would like to have my daughter's wedding before she is as big as her mother."

"Yes, sir. But the beatings, could you talk to Cameron?"

"What's he got to do with Alice?"

"Nothing as far as I know, but it's his people who're dishing out the beatings."

* * * *

There are a couple of private eyes who will wear makeup to cover their bruises. The only time I ever use makeup is if I'm undercover. So far, nothing in this case had forced me to that. But thinking about makeup reminded me that there were men who wore it and wanted to be desired by other men. Some of them wanted to be women. Others liked the way makeup and women's clothes felt on them.

I thought of Vic or Vicky Tomlinson. He is tall, blonde, and struts Sunset in Hollywood like a hooker on Saturday night. As far as I knew, he had nothing to do with this case, but he did know a lot about the sexual underground that extended from Hollywood, to the hills, and all the way to Malibu. He even knew what was happening up in San Francisco and Sacramento.

He stepped to my car and looked inside.

"Oh, you!" He was disappointed.

"Get in. I want to talk."

"You deign to be seen with me?"

"If you keep your hands to yourself."

"How much?"

"That depends on what you've got for me," I said.

"You and your information. When are you going to want something more from me? I would pay you to stick it in me. I really would. Or just to get my mouth around it."

"When hell freezes over. Get in."

I made a turn at the corner and kept moving east toward downtown. "What's going on with these murders?" I asked.

"Murders?"

"The Black Dahlia. What are you hearing?"

"You mean there's another one?"

"Tell me about the Dahlia."

"I have already told the police everything I know, which is exactly zero, *nada*, zip, nothing." He flipped his hands when he talked.

I drove a few more blocks without speaking and turned south on Western Avenue. I knew Vic before he was Vicky, and I knew that you asked him just one question and waited. Often, there were long pauses, but still you waited.

"Okay, you twisted my arm, you bully. There is some evil nastiness going on and for once it does not have a thing to do with Hollywood rich people, just crazy people, people who would boil their mother in oil if they wanted to get rid of her. They have heard that Los Angeles is the place for that. I swear somebody must be advertising in the *Saturday Evening Post*."

I turned on Olympic Boulevard and headed West. For his protection, I was driving on streets where neither of us was known.

I wondered if anyone in the LAPD knew anything about this, and if they did, what were they doing about it? I wanted to ask Vicky for names, but I knew I would get them in due time. He always gave me information. Whether the information was good or if I could use it, was for me to decide.

"They had a party at the Roosevelt Hotel on Saturday night and I hear it was a good one. Beautiful women, I mean real women. Men hung like fire hoses and depravity like you cannot believe. It went on all night long. A party like that going on the night poor little Cinderella Smart got all chopped up in little pieces too. I can't believe it."

"How do you know about it?"

"You must know that I would crash a party like that."

I didn't think that Trugante and Cameron would let someone like Vicky to crash their party. Neither would the Roosevelt, but there were always back doors and help from bellhops who never seem to get enough in tips.

"It was a veritable cornucopia of pleasure and pain, a profusion of beauty and ugliness, a plethora of the sweet and the tart. But poor Elizabeth, she did not know what she walked into. Do you know... Of course you don't. You are so wrapped up in bullshit that–" He sniffled. "Poor Cinderella."

He took a dainty handkerchief from his padded brassiere, and touched his nose. It was the first time I had heard Elizabeth Short called "Cinderella." I wanted to ask questions, like what did Elizabeth Short have to do with Laura Prendergast or Laura Fane, but from experience I knew I would learn more from him by just listening.

"There were beautiful girls and strange men at that party. And there were people who had keys to an interesting little house in the hills. Ricky, you would not believe what goes on in this town. I know that you know there are bastards who would hurt you just for the pleasure of hearing you squeal, but I am coming to learn that there are people who want to be hurt as well. Can you believe that? People who *want* to be hurt! Oh, God, not me. Sometimes it is painful when – oh, you know, but after a while it... Oh, my! Maybe I do understand."

He was beating all around God's little acre, and he wasn't telling me anything that I didn't know.

"There was one, the last one, they sold her to the highest bidder. But the bidder let her go. Actually let her go. Some say he did it to protect her. Can you imagine such a thing? I don't know who she was, but they say she was somebody important or rich or some other some such. Thank God for her that she got out of it. I mean, I know she got out of it because I saw her on the street a day or two later."

As I looked straight ahead, I felt my jaws tighten. If he was talking about Laura, she didn't keep out of it, but Vicky didn't know that.

"Oh, dear. She didn't get out of it, did she?"

I did not respond.

"It just goes to show you what an awful, evil town Los Angeles is – not to mention Hollywood. Those people, they..."

He continued to babble about evil, never recognizing that he was part of it – or maybe we all are. I try not to judge, but sometimes I do it in spite of myself. After a while, I was tired of listening to a sermon that did not seem to be going anyplace.

"What was the name of the girl, the one they sold at the party?"

That stopped him dead, and he sulked. I should have let him go on.

"Okay, if you have to be *so* nosy. Her name was Laura something. Used to be an extra at MGM"

"And the name of the guy who bought her?"

"You mean the first time?"

"Both times."

"Well, I only know about the first time. I don't know his name, but what I do know is that the old man who bought her first was an absolute gentleman. He even treated *me* like a lady, and you know how difficult it is for some people to do that. He was sweet. I liked him."

"How do you know he let her go?

"Because she was right back in the clutches of those people again. Mister Cameron sold her a second time and she ran away. She said she was going home to daddy or some such. I saw her on Sunset. Some fellow tried to pick her up in a car and she ran away from him, but right back into the clutches of those people. I don't know why she didn't go back to her husband the way she said she was."

"You talked to her?"

"Aren't you listening? She said her husband called her names, 'whore' and 'tramp' and things like that, but she said that was minor compared to what was happening to her since she left him. The people who seemed to own her were just so vicious – not the little man in the funny hat, but the others. I *do* think they are connected with organized vice, do you know?"

I knew.

"Do you know that that there was a woman there who actually tried to hire me for a house of some such. She said they would pay me well, but you know me, Ricky. I am my own woman. I make my own living. And very frankly, I do not like it when someone hurts me just for the sake of hurting me."

"Do you know the name of the woman who tried to hire you?"

"A woman in a blonde wig is all I know, although I met her at the party."

"Was she with anyone?"

"I think she was with *every*one. But you know me, Ricky dear, I am a one-man woman – at least one man at a time."

Yes, I knew him, poor bastard. I wondered what goes on in a person's childhood, or even in his wiring, that short-circuits a brain like that. I took him back to Highland Avenue near his personal showcase on Hollywood Boulevard, and I slipped him twenty dollars.

"For that I'll give you anything you want? I would do anything for you, Ricky. Absolutely *any*thing!" he said.

"Then see what else you can learn."

"Oh, you!"

Someone pulled Vicky away from my car. I thought it was a cop, but it turned out to be Little Georgie.

"Page, I need your help," he said. He opened the door and climbed in.

"Oh my, you are just running a veritable taxi service," Vicky said, and he – she – whatever crossed the street and strutted toward Grauman's Chinese Theater.

CHAPTER XVII

"What're doing with that faggot?" Little Georgie asked as I pulled away from the curb.

"You never know," I said. I would rather him think I was queer than give up one snitch to another. "You look like you haven't slept in a month."

"I got people after me," Georgie said.

"Sold a money wheel to the wrong couple?"

"Nothin' to do with money wheels. I got cabbies out looking for me."

"Skip out on a fare?"

"You ain't funny, so don't try to be."

I turned east on Franklin. I've learned from experience that people do not usually look into cars unless they're hookers or looking for someone specific. From the wide-eyed disheveled look of Little Georgie, I figured he wanted to be with almost anybody he trusted.

"I gotta get out of town," he said.

"I hope don't expect me to drive you."

"Just to Union Station. Can you lend me a few bucks?"

"What did you do?"

"Not sure, but every damn pimp and cabbie in L.A. is tryin' to track me down."

"Which pimps?"

"You think I keep a roster? A pimp is a pimp. You gonna give me a lift to the station or not?"

"Have I turned around yet?"

"Okay, smart guy. Thanks."

"What are they after you for?"

"I must've given the wrong scoop to the wrong guy. Lucky I got some people who like me or I'd already be hangin' up by my thumbs."

His choice of words make me think about Laura Prendergast.

"Who did you scoop?"

"Some cop. He knows some pimps. He's the one after me."

"What about the cabbies?"

"They're all working together, but damned if I know how or why. It ain't all cabbies though. Just a couple."

"But you don't know who's after you?"

"Somebody from downtown, not Hollywood. At least I don't think Hollywood. I been givin' out stories on the Dahlia and somebody don't like it."

"What d'ya know about the Dahlia?"

"Nothing. I'm makin' 'em up. I took a wild ass guess that the cabbie that got killed the other day was tied up in it because he knew where the action was."

"So that's how it got into the papers."

"It was a reporter friend. She wanted somethin' so I give it to her. She give me twenty bucks – not like some other pikers I know."

"Do you have a name for this big spender?"

He told me and I remembered the byline article in the Sun. It wasn't a full story, just a part of one that was well off the lead article. I didn't think it was worth following because it was about the Dahlia and not Laura. Now, I knew that Little Georgie made it up. I wondered how many other false rumors were out there.

"Did you find Laura Prendergast yet?" he asked as we rode a bit farther. I wondered if he was fishing for information or verifying something that he had picked up.

"No," I said.

"A hundred bucks could take me a long way. Look, there's this pimp that's got guys on the street. He's spreading out. I think he's trying to set up a place in Beverly Hills."

I wondered where a street snitch like Georgie would pick up that kind of information. "You making that story up too?"

"I talked to some of those girls. He's promisin' the moon."

"Do you know who this big connection is?"

"Not yet. Could be Trugante, Cameron, or Billy Bennett, even somebody new who's paying off the hats, but I don't know about anybody new tryin' to set up."

I still did not believe that the kind of hookers Georgie would run into would be of any interest to Trugante or Cameron or even Billy Bennett, who ran a discreet little place in the Hollywood Hills.

"Did somebody sic you on me?"

"What d'ya mean?"

I didn't reply. "What time's your train leave?"

"Beats me. I'm gettin' the first one east."

"No luggage."

"I'll get some on the way," he said. Which meant he would try to eye somebody about his size coming in and pick up their bags when they weren't looking. "Come on Rick. I done a lot for you. A hundred bucks could save my life."

A hundred wasn't likely, but I'd probably slip him ten before it was all over. Being a private eye was getting to be an expensive proposition, but I could get the money back on expenses.

"What else do you know about this cop?"

"The only thing I know about him, is that I never heard of him before."

"Name?"

"No name, but he's a big guy, broad shoulders. He almost nailed me on Sunset last night. I had to hide in a damn alley. He was after me all right."

"Who?"

"Told ya, a cop I don't know. They say he was working up in the valley before he got here."

If he were one of the ones who messed me up, Georgie would know them from the Hollywood beat.

There was far more to L.A. prostitution than just Trugante, Cameron and Billy Bennett. There were a dozen souls controlling the streets in Hollywood, hundreds in L.A. County, and there were new ones coming in all the time. The ones who paid protection got to stay.

"Where'd you get the cab driver story?"

"Told you, I made it up."

I glanced over at him and saw that he was staring straight ahead.

"How did you tie in the dead driver with the Dahlia?"

"Somebody wanted a story and I gave it to 'em. It ain't much of a story if it's not about the Dahlia. Besides, nobody even knows that Laura Prendergast is missing." He said it in the present tense, which meant that Sandiri and the LAPD had covered it up in the streets as well as in the paper.

"Did you tell this reporter that Laura Prendergast was missing?"

"If I said it, she'd find a way to use it. You know me, Rick. I got that from you. A good snitch don't pass on stories he gets from his best customers."

His going-away present just went from ten to twenty dollars.

"Any idea where you're going?"

"East. St. Louis maybe."

"Cold this time of the year."

"Well, I damn sure ain't gonna go to Kansas City."

The Kansas City mob, like the Chicago mob had connections to Los Angeles, probably to Trugante.

"Just drive past the station to make sure there ain't no goons out front. Then drop me off on Main. I might be able to pick up a bag on the street."

At the next traffic signal, I took a twenty from my wallet and gave it to him.

"Can't work the hundred, huh?"

"I don't have a money wheel."

L.A.'s Union Station looks like a California Mission. If there weren't so many cabs out front, with people going and coming with luggage, you might think it was the busiest church in America. We drove by and I helped Georgie look for goons who might be waiting for him in particular, but the chances that Georgie was valuable enough for anybody to glue a man to Union station was remote.

"Look me up if you come back," I said and I gave him my card.

"You're okay, Mister Page."

"Yeah," I said, and he got out of the car. I wasn't sure if he had ever called me 'Mister' before.

Not many people who knew Georgie would be good to him, and God knew that I didn't like some of the cons he ran, but he was a good snitch. And if there was such a thing as honor between a snitch and his client, Georgie had it with me. I can't say he had the same trust with the Sun reporter.

On my way back to Hollywood, I thought about the card I had just given him and chuckled. I was sure the little son of a bitch would find a way to make money with it.

* * * *

As I stepped into the lobby of the Tower on Sunset, both the desk clerk and Mickey Wren looked at me. Instead of going to the desk, I went straight to Mickey and sat in one of the lobby easy chairs across a small table from him.

Mickey grinned. "You bruise nice."

"Would you tell Mister Cameron that I have permission from Mister Trugante to talk to him again."

"Did you really see me with Two-Ton Tony?"

"Every punch."

"I thought that was you. Didn't you learn from last time?"

"Learn what?"

"To leave Mister Cameron alone."

It was the way his mind went: here, there, and everywhere. I was the guy who had been flattering him the last couple of days, but I was also the guy who was bugging his boss, and he had trouble working that out.

"Don't you get messages?" he said. "Most people get messages."

He wasn't talking about an answering service. He had refocused on me as the enemy.

"Didn't I just tell you that Mister Trugante said it was okay for me to talk to him."

"I work for Mister Cameron."

"But Cameron works for Mister Trugante."

He squinted, trying to piece together the simple bit of information I had thrown at him. His brain was so scrambled from getting off the canvas too many times and going right back down, that even the simplest logic escaped him. For just an instant, I thought about my own beatings, and I wondered if that's where my brain was headed.

"Call upstairs and ask Mister Cameron if I can see him."

While he went to the desk, I thought about Laura Prendergast hanging from ankles and wrists, and I thought about the Dahlia's rope burns.

"He says I come up and make you two a couple of drinks. He says that you are okay today."

"Just today?"

"That's what he said."

I didn't think that Cameron knew how casually Mickey put out information, and I wasn't about to tell him.

When we reached the apartment, Cameron shook my hand vigorously. We sat in the same two chairs as a few days ago. I sunk into the sofa again, and he was all smiles and affability. We had barely finished talking about the weather when Mickey brought us our drinks. He was a jack-of-all-trades and a master of non-lethal violence. Non-lethal so far, that is.

"What happened to you was a terrible mistake. Mickey here mistook you for another person – isn't that right, Mickey?"

"Yes, sir. Another person."

I tasted my Scotch.

"You seem to have an interest in a woman who used to work for me. A Miss Dixie Joy?"

"How would you know that?"

"She seems to be a permanent fixture at the Hollywood Vista. She's not doing night work anymore, I understand. How is she doing?"

"I thought you knew Trugante well enough to know that she's working for him."

"Well, yes, but I don't see her very often."

"She's doing fine. It's me that's not doing so well." I touched the bruises on both cheeks.

"I *am* sorry about that. I neglected to communicate to Mickey and his friends that you're all right, a friend in fact."

"Any friend of Sal's is a friend of yours?"

"Exactly."

I believed that like I believed that it never rained in Los Angeles.

"Isn't that true, Mickey?"

"You said it, Mister C," Mickey said, which was not the same as agreeing. I doubted that he was even following the conversation.

"Terrible about these murders here in Los Angeles," he said.

"Murders?"

"The Black Dahlia, of course. And the cab driver. They say a woman did that but how they could know that is totally beyond my comprehension. Black Dahlia, a terrible case. Chopped that poor girl in half. Sex. I'm sure it was sex."

He was talking quickly and in choppy sentences. Maybe Trugante had called ahead and he was trying to make amends, but he was definitely nervous.

"You let a man buy sex freely, and things like that don't happen. Men who are getting it regularly don't go crazy and, Mister Page, you don't know how much it hurts me to hear about things like that happening."

"Lots of rumors. Some even say she wasn't a prostitute," I said.

"What do you know about the case?" He leaned forward and opened his eyes wide as if he expected me to drop a gem of detail about the Dahlia.

"Just what I read in the papers."

"But I understand that you have friends inside the LAPD?"

"I understand that you do too," I said.

He frowned. "Oh, yes, the other night. I am sure you can understand how terribly sorry I am about that."

"And the Santa Monica pier?"

"What about the Santa Monica pier?"

"Ask Mickey."

"Do you know anything about that, Mickey?"

"I like the Ferris Wheel, Mister C."

"Why did you throw me off the pier?" I asked looking across to Mickey. He was at a modified parade rest posture at the bedroom door, standing guard.

"I didn't do that."

"But you knew about it?"

"I heard about it," he said, with no inflection. He wanted to look to Cameron for help, but he knew he shouldn't. He was afraid to talk about it, maybe afraid that his lies would not hang together. I was sure he had that problem from time to time.

"Who was the woman with you when you threw me off the pier?"

Mickey looked at Cameron, who could hold out no longer.

"I'm sure that if Mickey saw someone throw you off the pier he would have reported it to the police – wouldn't you, Mickey?"

"Yes, sir. And I didn't see no woman on the pier either."

"You know, Page, you are very tenacious. I could use a man like you. I am sure you're not working every day for your twenty-five dollars. I can give you a hundred and fifty dollars a week, cash and you wouldn't have to worry about finding clients. You might even enjoy bodyguard work."

"What about me, Mister C?"

"And I don't have to tell you that in the business I'm in there would be side benefits you would never get working for the Pinkertons."

"I don't work for the Pinkertons."

"Figure of speech. What do you say?"

"Thanks for the offer, but I prefer working alone."

"What about me Mister C?" Mickey was offended.

"You are well taken care of, Mickey. We would never leave you out in the cold. Did you have any luck following up on the Merriman fellow?"

"Following up?" I raised my eyebrows.

"After he slipped you in Santa Monica."

"He slipped me in Santa Monica?"

"When we threw–"

Mickey caught himself from saying it, but he had already put his fists together over his head and brought them down hard like Patty Drake must have looked when she slugged me with the frying pan. Then he quickly shifted his eyes to Cameron's.

"When what?" I asked.

Cameron nodded his permission.

"When Miss Drake hit you over the head."

"How did you know about that?"

"She told us," Cameron said, interrupting. He thought I had heard enough from Mickey, and that I had figured out most of the truth.

"It wasn't Miss Drake on the pier. Who was it?" I said.

"That's enough, Page!"

Cameron held his gaze on mine, but he also held a smile.

"That's all waves under the pier, Mister Page, Rick. May I call you Rick? It's time for us to cooperate. Mister Trugante is looking for a new son-in-law and it is up to you to pick one for him."

He might have guessed that from the questions I had asked the other day, but he seemed quite certain of my mission. I didn't think this was something Trugante would discuss with Cameron or anyone else who didn't have a need to know. I didn't bother to ask how Cameron knew, because all I would get was more lies.

He leaned back in his chair. "Have you found Missus Prendergast yet?" he asked.

I shook my head. "Do you have any ideas?"

"None, but I assure you that I haven't seen her."

"That lady they found cut in half?" Mickey asked.

"A different lady, Mickey."

"What if they find her like that lady?" he asked.

"Mickey, Mickey. How do you come up with such ideas? I'm afraid Mickey gets conversations mixed up. I have an ongoing interest in that case. Often Mickey overhears my conversations and–"

"I think it's awful what happened to her, Mister C."

"Yes."

"They should find the killer and string him up by his heels."

"Enough."

Mickey's lines seemed rehearsed or at the very least, mimicked.

"That's a real puzzler," I said. I wanted to keep the subject going, but my act wasn't good enough.

"Yes, a real puzzler. I suppose we are finished here?"

Cameron stood and offered his hand across the cocktail table.

"If you have anymore questions, please give me a call. I am always happy to help Mister Trugante. Mickey, will you see that Mister Page gets safely to his car?"

"Why did you throw me off the pier?" I asked Mickey again.

Cameron sighed and waved me back to the sofa. "We might as well get this straightened out. I'm certain you'll be bothering poor Mickey until we do."

CHAPTER XVIII

I waved off a second drink because I did not expect this to be a very long story – I didn't expect it to be a true story either.

"Do you want to tell him, Mickey?"

"Me?" Mickey looked frightened. He looked at me and licked his lips. Then he looked away from me. He quickly told how he had followed me to Santa Monica, saw me take Merriman, and how Patty conked me with the frying pan at the beach-front.

"We thought you was dead. So we took you out to the pier and we tossed you."

I looked at Cameron and shook my head.

"Patty is a friend of mine," Cameron said. "Mickey was trying to protect her. And she was just trying to protect that kid boyfriend of hers. There's no reason for anybody to go to jail. You don't think so, do you, Mister Page?"

"We thought you was dead," Mickey said again. He said it enthusiastically, but he was no actor.

"And a couple of Hollywood cops were involved?"

"No, no. Just me and Merriman and Miss Drake," Mickey said. It was a lie, rehearsed and set up because they figured I couldn't remember. The two Hollywood cops were definitely with him, but I did not think that either Merriman or Patty Drake was.

"They thought you were dead," Cameron said. I heard it three times, but that didn't make it the truth.

"And outside the Hollywood Vista Motel? Did you think I was dead? Is that why you beat the shit out of me?" I said it straight to Mickey.

"No need to go filthy-mouthed, Mister Page," Cameron said. "I told you. Mickey mistook you for another person. When a gentleman goes with one of my girls, I do not expect that checks made out to cash will bounce."

"Who was this person who had a bounced check? Did he look like me?" I was angry. I felt that I had the support of Trugante, but maybe I should be more careful. I was glad that I didn't have a second Scotch.

"I don't reveal my clients' names, even if they do bounce checks," he said.

Cameron had coached Mickey well, and they were now shoveling it by the truckload, one lie on top of another on top of another. So many lies that Cameron hoped it was impossible for me to sort out the truth.

"I assure you it will not happen again," Cameron said. "Mickey. Take a good look at this man. You are never to bother him again."

"Yes, Mister C, but what if–"

"There are no 'what ifs!' Mister Page, thank you. I wish you the best of luck in finding Mrs. Prendergast."

His comment led me to think that Mickey and the two cops had followed me from Prendergast's place. I asked about that, and Mickey looked genuinely confused.

"We was waiting at the motel," he said.

I think he was telling the truth, but if he was, who was following me?

"Mickey, will you go hold an elevator for Mister Page?"

Mickey moved quickly into the hall. I had a sense that it was a recurring scene when Cameron wanted a few things said out of the earshot of his flunky. He started to talk while Mickey went for the elevator.

"I understand that the police are getting close to the Dahlia killer. I was wondering, with your connections at the LAPD, could you let me know how that's coming along? It's worth a thousand dollars to me."

"Was Elizabeth Short one of your girls?"

"She worked for a rival. I'd love to pin it on him."

I had heard that she was just an ordinary girl out to have fun, but that was the newspaper story.

"Who?" I asked.

"No matter," he said.

It did matter, I thought, and he wanted me to pump him. Whatever he said would be a lie or at least misleading, so I let it slide and started for the door.

* * * *

I remembered that the first time I talked to Cameron that he said the guy he saw with Laura had a nice suit. Now I thought about Prendergast's butler, Albert. He was small, in his fifties – maybe the exact kind of person to wear a bowler hat.

Among the things that Cameron and Mickey told me about, and based on how they acted, what struck me as most true was Mickey did not follow me from Prendergast's place. The maid had let me out of the house, not Albert, and I wondered if Albert could have been the one following me. If he did, was it for him or for Prendergast?

The more I thought about the whole business, the more I wished I had let Cameron drop the shoe about who might be his rival – or maybe I was afraid to hear it. Before I started this case, I thought that prostitution had only three sources: whorehouses, street hookers and call girls. I was sure that Trugante would think of some of his places as "Houses of Ill Repute" or bordellos. Cameron ran an "escort service." Whore houses and call girls, but not street hookers – at least not officially.

It was after dark and I thought about Dixie and last night. I hardly talked to her because I was so out of it. There were other things that I could do now, but only one I really wanted to do.

I called her at the Hollywood Vista and the desk clerk connected me. I was about the hang up when Dixie came on the line and told me to come over.

* * * *

"You certainly do leave an awful mess in the bathroom," Dixie said when I stepped into her room.

"I'm not sure that I was a hundred percent together when I left here this morning. Sorry."

She put her fingers on my chin. She turned my face to one side, then to the other. "You are still rather bruised up. Does it hurt?"

"I'm tough but bruises don't heal overnight."

"You are that, but I'd better dab it with some more alcohol," she said, and she grinned. I loved it when she did the "ah" for "I" and the "aw" for "are" thing.

"No you won't."

She patted me on the cheek, then pecked me on the lips. "How would you like to take me to dinner?"

"I've been thinking about that for a while. Do you know Musso and Frank?" I asked her.

"I do not know them personally, but I do know their place. Near Las Palmas, right?"

"That's the one."

Compared to a lot of places we could go, Musso and Frank was pricey, but they had a good menu and star clientele. I always wore a jacket and tie, whether I was working or not. She must have just come from Trugante's because she was still in her business suit. We fit the place just fine.

A waiter in tuxedo tried to avoid looking at my bruises, but he didn't do a very good job of hiding his disgust. He led us to a booth in a near corner of the restaurant where few would look. He sat me with my back to the rest of the place. I think his idea was that people would not notice me and especially not my bruises.

111

Three other tables and one booth were occupied. In the middle of the room, Lucille Ball was sitting with a Latin looking guy who must be her husband. I couldn't remember his name and I asked Dixie.

"Desi Arnaz. He has a rumba band or somethin'. She starred in the last picture that I ever appeared in. I will never forget that. Can you imagine gettin' paid to do the *Two O'Clock Jump* to Harry James – along with a couple dozen other boys and girls of course. If you see that movie, you can see me dance."

"You like to dance?"

"I just love it."

"The Palladium's right across the street from my office."

"I know that, and I would love for you to take me sometime." She was hitting me with those "ahs" again.

She ordered a martini, a drink I wasn't crazy about, and I settled on Scotch with a little ice. When I looked up from the menu, Red Skelton was coming in. It must be redhead night.

"Did you find the daddy-to-be for Alice yet?"

I decided not to answer.

"He is really pissin' in his grits about that one."

I hadn't told Trugante anything yet, and I had a sense that she was trying to draw information from me. He would learn it from me when I was ready to tell him. Or when he was ready to beat it out of me. I damn sure wasn't going to let him hear it from Dixie.

"How about Merriman?" she said.

I didn't know how she knew about him. She was still trying to draw me out and I was getting angry. When the waiter brought our drinks, she dropped that subject and talked about her time in the movies some more.

"That address you gave me was an empty house."

"Empty?"

"Not a stick of furniture – not even in the basement. You two were pretty close, weren't you?"

She looked down into her martini. If she showed any emotion, I didn't see it. Finally, she sighed. "Good friends, yes, very good friends. She should have learned to type."

"And take shorthand," I said. "But being married to somebody like Prendergast couldn't be all bad."

"Hmmm." It had an editorial sound to it.

"It was that bad?" I asked.

"She could hardly leave a room without him checkin' on her and she was not allowed to leave the house alone. It is no wonder she ran away from the son of a bitch." She dragged out the "son of a bitch."

She sipped her martini again. It was half-gone.

"No luck finding her yet?"

"Not a stick." I finally tasted my Scotch.

"Are you sure you went to the right place?"

By the time the waiter took our order, Dixie was ready for another martini. She was quietly furious that I was asking questions and would tell her nothing.

"Sounds like you don't like Prendergast."

She didn't answer.

"Why did she go back to hooking?"

"She wasn't hookin'. Not the last time I talked to her."

"You talked to her after you saw her at the Roosevelt?"

"On the telephone. When she gave me the address."

She had already finished her martini. She pulled the olive from the toothpick and sucked out the pimento. She seemed to savor it as she looked into my eyes. I didn't know if it was a sex thing, a way to avoid further question, or both. Finally she bit the olive and chewed. I was doing the eye business back at her and she beat me to the next questions.

"Are you tryin' to get something on her? Maybe get some grounds for divorce, or an annulment that will leave her out in the cold like just any girl on the street?"

"I'm trying to find her," I said.

Her murder was not in the papers and Prendergast seemed as pleased as anyone to keep it from public knowledge. I didn't want it out either. What I didn't understand was why Cameron didn't know about it since he had a couple of Hollywood cops working for him.

"It does not seem right that the house was empty. She clearly told me that she was stayin' there."

"If I saw her, she'd be back with Prendergast by now."

"I am quite seriously doubt that. She hated that man."

"Was she into any kind of unusual sex? Masochism, for example?"

She raised her chin as if she didn't know what I was talking about. Then she looked across the room and watched as the waiter brought her new martini to the table. I expected her to plunge into it as she had done with the first, but this time, she just played with the toothpick and the olive.

"You told me that there was some kind of convention at the Roosevelt. The hotel says no."

"It was a private convention, arranged by Mister Cameron."

In Cameron's business, that made sense.

"You are quite the shamus. Where does that come from anyhow, that 'shamus' business?"

"Some writer, I suppose. I never knew a private detective who thought of himself that way. What did the guy who left with her look like?"

"Is this some kind of test? I already told you, he was little, old, and with gray hair."

"Hat?"

"I didn't see a hat. They were gettin' ready to leave as we came through the lobby."

"Did you and Trugante go to the same party?"

"It was not a party – it was a convention."

I tasted my Scotch. I was getting impatient at Dixie because she was getting testy with her answers.

"Rick, please, don't speak to me of Mister Trugante's business."

"It wasn't a convention of inventors was it?"

"If you ask another question along this line, I will leave. What would Mister Trugante say if he knew you were askin' me about his business?"

"I thought it was Cameron's business."

"He was caterin' for Mister Trugante. Rick, please. I came here with you because I like you, but I am beginnin' to think that you like me only for the information you can get from me."

She was right, that was exactly what I was doing – pumping for information. I wanted other things too, the companionship, of course, and later the sex.

We ate with little talk, but with a lot of smiles and looks, some of apology. If she was seen on the arm of Trugante, she might be special to him and it might be smart of me to back out of anything that had to do with her. But if she was special to Trugante, she should have told me. If she didn't, he might, and it would not be pleasant. I might lose not only a fee, but I would be subject to another beating or worse. How many warnings can a guy get?

"Are you Trugante's girl?"

She stopped forking her salmon and looked up. "No," she said. She pursed her lips ugly.

"That makes you mad?" I asked.

"It makes me angry that you believe I am not a good secretary."

"I have no way to judge that, but why wouldn't you be?"

"It is not funny."

"I didn't say it was."

"You were laughing at me?"

She lowered her fork in her plate and glared. "Sal and Michael have their choice of girls who are younger and prettier than I am. I am a woman who has been through that particular mill and I do not like the fact that you are tryin' to grind me up in it all over again."

"Sorry," I said. I had begun to like her, and her indignation added a touch to her personality that made me like her even more.

In a few minutes, we settled on a more civil conversation about how good the food was. By that time, a dozen other people had come into the place. At three tables, there were movie stars, and we discussed their pictures. I have a keen ear for what goes on at other tables. I was not within earshot of any of the stars, but those who were not stars seemed to be having the same conversations as Dixie and me about those who were.

When we returned to her motel room, she whipped the coat off my shoulders, pinned my arms, and pushed me down on the bed. Her mouth was all over mine. Her fingers reached first for my gun to toss it on the floor, then for my belt. While she did that, I slipped out of my new shoulder holster and dropped it to the floor.

I was kissing and tugging just as she was. I wanted her as much as she wanted me, maybe even more. I was in too much pain to enjoy it last night, but I could overlook the pain now.

We still had most of our clothes on when we made love the first time. The second time, the foreplay was a slow undressing of each other. We were caressing and kissing this, that, and everything else, things I had learned overseas. By now, every starlet and prostitute, and maybe some housewives, had learned it too, but I was reciprocating.

It was like Paris all over again, but this time it was free and full and emotional. I liked her and I liked the way she dug her nails into my back like the claws of a tiger and I liked the way she growled through clenched teeth. And after a while, it was more than Paris was. It had nothing to do with price or physical pleasure and so much more to do with the way I was beginning to feel about her and the way she seemed to feel about me.

We had a drink and we made love again. It was a good way to prepare for a full night of deep sleep, my first in a long time.

At seven in the morning, Dixie woke me and I was still groggy, maybe even groggier than usual. I was ready for an encore, but she handed me the phone instead. I had barely heard it ringing.

CHAPTER XIX

"It's for you," she said, disgusted.

I took the phone and listened to the girl from my answering service: "You told me not to bother you unless it was very important. The note here says 'unless very, very important.'"

"And I meant it," I said.

"You don't have to get mad, but this fellow calls about an hour ago and says that you are to go to this address. I just took the note. I figured you would call. But he calls just now and asks if I gave you the address yet, and when I said no, he jumps down my throat, you know, real mean like. So, I said I'd call you right away. So here's the address–"

"What did he sound like?" I asked, interrupting her.

"Very polite the first time, but the last time? Wow. I mean he was biting my head off. I don't like it when–"

"What was the address?"

"Uh, oh, yeah. It was, here it is." She gave me an address only a few blocks from my own place. I fumbled for a pencil and asked for the number again. "Did he give an apartment number?"

"No, sir. He just said to look in the basement bedroom."

"That doesn't sound right."

"'Basement bedroom' is what he said."

"Thanks," I said and I hung up. I felt groggier than when I went to sleep.

"What was that?"

"Work."

"I thought you could never work for anyone else."

"Except clients. Can I use your shower?"

"If you clean up after. I suppose this means that we aren't going to spend the day together?"

"Maybe later," I said.

I was still showering when I realized that it was already Saturday. It was probably time for me to get Merriman's name to Trugante, but first things first.

Messages like, "look in the basement bedroom," had a way of being important.

* * * *

The apartment building around the corner from my place was four stories high and maybe thirty yards wide. I think the architecture was called classic Castilian, but the place was far from classic now. The stucco front had been painted many times and the paint was coming off in flecks here and there. Like my own building, it was once occupied by stars or near stars, but that was at a time when actors had barely started talking on screen and many still lived in Hollywood.

When I knew what I was looking for, I usually managed to get into a building without help. In this case, there would be too many doors to open, too many people to surprise, and too much noise to make without somebody calling the cops. I located the super and asked to see the basement bedroom. We talked as he took me downstairs in the elevator.

"You are in luck, my friend. The fellow who lives in that room, he has left us." He spoke with a slight Mexican accent.

"Where did he go?"

"He said he was going back to the east. Hollywood, it is too hot for him, he said."

"What did he mean by that?"

"He was in some trouble with the police, I think. I think he was always in trouble with the police."

We walked along a dark tunnel of bedsprings, mattresses and old furniture.

"There is a toilet and shower down the hall. These, we will share."

He had the impression that I wanted to rent the room, and I let him keep thinking it.

"I have been away for a few days, and the place is not yet clean, but we will get that done for you very quickly," he said. He put the key in the lock.

"When did the previous tenant tell you he was leaving?"

"He did not tell me. He told the owner of the building. This fellow tried to get some rent returned to him. It is not possible, of course. You pay for full month or a full week. No refunds. I make that clear now."

The room was darker than the hallway and there were no windows to give light. The super waved his arm around trying to find the pull string in the middle of the room.

"Mister Frommer, you are still here," he said and he pulled the string.

"*Madre de Dios!*" The super crossed himself as he bolted from the room.

"Jesus Christ," I said, groaning.

117

In the middle of the bed, still in his Hawaiian shirt and khaki slacks, was the trussed-up body of Little Georgie.

He was on his stomach, with his feet and wrists knotted together with clothesline. His body formed the same triangle that I had seen with the body of Laura Prendergast. Instead of hanging from the ceiling, he was lying on a bed. He was gagged with what I think was a man's sock. His throat was sliced from ear to ear. Blood had spilled over the bare mattress and onto the floor from the numerous slashes that were cut though his shirt and trousers to his flesh.

Except that he was fully clothed, the placement of Little Georgie's body was identical to Laura's.

I looked away from what had once been Georgie and looked around the room that was no bigger than ten by twelve. The dresser was piled with stuff, including five money wheels and a short stack of pulp western magazines. Without touching, I looked at the railroad ticket that lay in the middle of a chipped dinner plate. The destination was San Francisco, with yesterday's date. He was frightened enough that he had tried to mislead everybody into believing he was going east, or maybe he just didn't have enough money for another ticket.

Just as he had feared, someone had seen him going into Union Station. They had escorted him back here. I could think of no other explanation.

I looked across the body to the Hawaiian shirts and army khakis, clothes that hung on hooks in the wall. An easy chair was next to the bed with a movie magazine open across the arm. There was a chest of drawers, which I did not touch. In fact, I didn't touch anything. Just as he said, he was leaving in a hurry, and he had left his belongings – even his money wheels.

Only when I started to move did I realize that the puddle of blood under the bed had expanded and it was under the soles of my shoes. If I tried to go, I would leave a trail of bloody footprints. I lived too close to this place to try to get out before the police came. The super had seen me on the street and might even know where I lived. If I left, it would be only a matter of time before the cops would be knocking at my door, so I waited.

I heard the voices of people coming down the stairs. The last thing I noticed before I stepped out of the room was that someone had slashed the ass-end of Georgie's trousers.

I waited and two uniformed cops came down the hall through the clutter.

"Can't you afford no more bulbs down here?" one cop said.

"Electricity, it is expensive," said the super.

"Cheap Mexican landlords," the second cop said. When he reached me, he did a double take. "Ain't you the guy that got beat up over at the Hollywood Vista the other night?"

He was the one who had arrived after the beating.

"That's me."

"You got something to do with this?"

"Not much."

"Yeah, I'll bet – Jesus Christ!"

"My exact words."

"What the hell is this?"

The other cop, probably a rookie, looked into the room. He turned away, but before he could run, he threw up through one of the bedsprings that were leaning against the wall outside the room.

"Is there a phone down here someplace?" the first cop asked.

"I show you." The super was happy to get away from the blood-soaked bedroom.

"Don't you go anyplace. And you watch him." As soon as he ordered the rookie cop to stay put, the rookie vomited again.

"I'll stay right here," I said.

I did not want to look back into the room, but I was drawn to it, not by fascination but because I wanted to see the knot in the rope. I didn't touch the rope, but I studied the knot. It was the same kind of knot used to truss and hang Laura, and the same kind of brand-new clothesline they used to hang her from the ceiling. The end looked as if it had been freshly cut. If there had been something in the ceiling to tie it to other than a bare electric cord, I think he would be hanging there.

There might be no connection between Laura Prendergast and the Black Dahlia, but there damn sure was a connection between Laura and Little Georgie. This case was wilder than the Dahlia, but I was betting that the world would never know of it or of Laura or of Georgie. Maybe because of Prendergast, maybe for some other reason, but these murders were definitely in the shadow of the Black Dahlia Case, and I didn't know how Sandiri could keep it out of the light.

The second cop was huffing and puffing by the time the first came back, but he still would not look into the room.

"It'll be a while," the first cop said to the rookie. "You wanna go up to the lobby or something?"

"Yeah." The rookie gurgled the word and hurried down the hall and ups the stairs.

The first cop started to ask me questions and I held up both hands for him to be quiet. "Let's just wait for the detectives."

"You know this guy?"

"Yeah," I said, but it was my last answer. He didn't like it and he didn't like the fact that I wouldn't talk to him anymore.

"I should've run you in the other night," he said. We started to make small talk because I wouldn't answer his pertinent questions.

It was Saturday afternoon, so it was almost an hour before Sandiri came down the hall with somebody from the crime lab.

"Aw, shit," he said.

"He won't talk," the one cop said.

"I'll talk to the detective," I said.

I gave Sandiri quick rundown of how I got down here in the first place. I started to tell him what I thought and he told me to keep my thoughts to myself for a while. He was right about that. There were too many ears around.

He had the same thoughts I did, because he looked up at the ceiling to see that the electric cord was the only place they could have hung Georgie. He looked around the room more closely than I did and the lab guy stayed in the hall.

"Saturday's my biggest night. Don't get much this early in the day though," Sandiri said.

Sandiri finished looking and he returned to the hall. "Go get 'em," he said to the lab guy. Then he turned to me. "You know this guy?"

He knew that I did, but he was trying to mislead everybody within earshot.

The cop interrupted. "He's a small-time con man."

"Rick?"

"He did snitches for me."

"You got your foot in it again."

"Yeah." I showed him the blood on my shoe. "You're a sick cookie. D'ya know that?"

"Should I lock him up, Sarge?"

"Nah. I'll take care of that. Why don't you take your pal there and get him cleaned up." The rookie had come back, but he didn't look in the room.

"Yes, sir."

"Sorry, Sarge," the rookie cop said to Sandiri.

"Is this your first meat?"

"Yes, sir," the rookie said. His hair was cut to the quick. I had the sense that he was an ex-marine who had never been in combat.

"If you're lucky, you won't see it again," Sandiri said.

"Come on," the first cop said.

They went to the stairs at end of the hall and Sandiri led me down among the pipes in the boiler room while the lab guy started to take pictures. In Hollywood, everybody made pictures.

I told Sandiri my moves step by step from the phone call. I gave him all the background I could think of, and he asked me what I thought about it.

"You say it wasn't a crazy guy," I said. "I say it is. And I say that even if these last two were different from the Dahlia, it's the same killers. No matter what their reasons, they *are* crazy."

"Same guys, plural, huh? I might open my mind on the Dahlia business, but I don't think so."

I just shrugged. He had far more experience with murder than I did. We talked for over an hour. Then a Hollywood detective talked to me. Finally, Sandiri asked me if I wanted to get something to eat.

"After that?"

"Sure after that. Come on. If you keep doing what you're doing, you're gonna see a lot of this."

"What do you mean doing what I'm doing?"

"Being a private eye in L.A., that's what I mean."

"Oh."

We took Sandiri's car, parked on a no-parking lot, and went into a joint called the Vine Dance near Hollywood Boulevard.

CHAPTER XX

I knew Sandiri had been here before but he still looked around the place at the decorative palm leaves, palm trees and bamboo walls. Every time I came in here, I thought about the fire at Boston's Coconut Grove during the war. I looked for all the exits before I ever sat down. I never smoked in there. Sandiri was probably thinking the same thing.

I mentioned it to the owner once, and he very casually told me that it *could* happen and that was why they didn't put lanterns or candles on the tables. It didn't make me any more comfortable.

"This has nothing to do with the Black Dahlia," Sandiri said.

"Okay."

According to the newspapers, Elizabeth Short was a nobody. Little Georgie was nobody either, but Laura Prendergast was the wife of a millionaire. Somebody somewhere should have picked up the news.

"I'm *glad* it has nothing to do with the Dahlia case," Sandiri said. "Maybe I can get to the bottom of this one."

"What do you mean, 'this one'?"

"I mean maybe I can find a killer. They'll be asking questions about the Dahlia until the next century and they still won't make an arrest."

"Why not?"

"Remember when I asked you to quit the Laura Prendergast case?"

"Yeah."

"I thought it was the same people then," he said.

"And now?"

"Now we got a guy, so maybe not. Maybe we can put at least one bastard in with the cyanide."

For a half hour he beat me to numbness with questions he had already asked, all the while throwing asides that if I kept stumbling into things that somebody would end up making me a suspect.

"There are already people in the department who don't trust you, and they might need a scapegoat," he said.

"Does everybody trust you?"

"*Touché*." He continued to warn me that I could not be treated like an ordinary citizen even if we were friends. "And you could get yourself killed," he added.

"Yeah, I worry about that too. So what should I do? Get a job as an usher at one of Sid Grauman's theaters?"

"Hell, no. You'd just find bodies in the seats and I don't want to deal with that." He huffed and tasted his coffee. He never drank alcohol on duty.

It was early, but I was already drinking Scotch. "So what do you want from me?"

"Help," he said.

"What?" He threw me with that one.

"Help. I need some help."

He paused to let it sink in, but I had a question. "I don't get it. What kind of help? You told me to get out and—"

"This is my case and only mine. They won't even put a street cop into plain clothes for me, and as far as I'm concerned, this one is bigger than the Dahlia. It goes higher and it reaches into more important bedrooms."

"Which is why they won't give you any help?"

"Yep. And that's where you come in."

"You're going to deputize me?"

"Not even the lieutenant could get away with that. The way I see it, we're crossing the same streets anyhow. Let me make a guess: Prendergast is paying you to find out who killed his wife."

"How'd you know that?"

"Christ, Rick, I'm a detective. I see things and that's what it adds up to. Did you tell Trugante you got a son-in-law for him yet?"

"Not yet."

"Better do it quick. You're running out of time."

"You told me—"

"Trust me. Now's the time. Get it to him while you still can."

"What do you mean while I still can?"

"Pay attention: somebody threw you off the Santa Monica Pier and then beat the shit out of you. People keep giving you addresses where you find dead bodies – how long do you think it's going to be before I find you tied up with a hole cut in *your* ass?"

"I hadn't exactly pictured it that way."

"Well, start picturing it, and you'll either work harder to get to the bottom of this, or you'll get the hell out of town."

I just looked at him.

"Sometimes it's best to cut and run," he said.

I shook my head a couple of times real quick.

"I didn't think so," he said. "What haven't you told me?"

I told him that Little Georgie had spread the newspaper rumor about a cab driver was tied in with the Dahlia. I gave him a quick rundown of what I had already found out for Trugante and Cameron and about how I thought they related. "And if you repeat that, I could end up in the Pacific with cement shoes this time," I said.

"Okay, I'm gonna trust you. You don't lie to me much, especially not about important things."

"Thanks for the vote of confidence," I said.

The waitress brought our open-face burgers smothered with fried pineapple.

If I helped him, I would be helping myself because I would get closer to the killer of Laura Prendergast. I knew how other private eyes did it. They accepted advances just like I did. I knew from experience that more than half of them failed at what they set out to do. Some I knew were happy to just take the money to the bank and sit on their asses or make a half-hearted attempt to do what needed to be done. Even some of the guys working for Pinkerton did that, but they were usually found out and were fired quick.

"Okay," Sandiri said. "I'm going to give you some stuff you don't know. Whoever is doing this thing is going about it all wrong."

"What do you mean?"

"Everybody and his uncle thinks if you kill enough people you kill off the possibility of detection, but that's wrong. With each person you murder, you double your chances of getting caught. Each murder means more clues. Unless the killer is trying to send a message to somebody, maybe somebody like you, the fact that the murder method is similar just calls attention to 'em. How I've managed to keep Laura Prendergast out of the papers is a miracle. Not even Prendergast is screaming – and that's another story altogether."

"He came to me because he didn't think the LAPD was doing enough."

"Okay. We can chalk one up for him– Is that what he said? We're not doing enough?"

"That's what he said."

That seemed to bother Sandiri. I saw him squinting and his eyes moved as if he were trying to figure out something. Finally, he nodded. "Okay, but he's still on my suspect list. We got two murders, similar murders. People trussed up, but not like pigs on a spit – and do you know why?"

I shook my head and continued to chew. The way Sandiri kept talking, he'd be lucky to finish his burger a week from Tuesday.

"Because he wanted to put them in pain. Think about that for a moment."

"I knew that!"

"And don't act like a rookie who thinks he knows it all."

"Was Laura Prendergast's back broken?" I asked.

"No. And I don't think your pal Georgie's was either. You saw the slit in the ass of his pants and the way Laura was hanging naked?" He finally took a bite of his burger.

"You don't have to explain."

He took a moment to finish chewing. "We're starting to see more of it. Sex with pain. Somebody gets the idea that it's fun and sexy as hell to torture somebody and maybe even to screw them when they're in pain. You getting it now?"

"The *Grand Guignol*."

"What's that?"

I told about the puppets in Paris, the beatings, the sadism, but it was just puppets on puppets. "Some of the guys told me that there were shows like that with real people too. I never saw it, never wanted to," I said.

"No, shit. That's probably where it came from. Everybody's coming back from the war with everything from souvenir Nazi armbands to gonorrhea. Some bastard gets into that and... I don't even want to talk about it."

"But you have to think about it." We both chewed for a while. Then I added, "But I damn sure don't understand it."

"This bastard, or bastards, get their stones rocked by that kind of thing. Ricky, you've led a sheltered life. Welcome to the world of California murder."

I just looked at him. I had just finished telling him what I heard about in Paris, and he was telling me that the monster had crossed the Atlantic and was alive in the Golden State. I just shook my head.

"You hang in here with this case, you keep getting yourself mixed up in these murders, and you're gonna see things you don't want to see. You'll learn things you don't want to learn. This is not gonna be a pig roast."

Considering the way the victims were trussed, I thought that was an unfortunate choice of words.

"And it'll get worse," he said.

"I don't see how."

"Because you've got no imagination." He returned to his burger.

Finding Little Georgie trussed up and murdered was an ugly way to spend a Saturday afternoon, and Sandiri was making it uglier with his stories of ugly crimes of the past. The only reason the Dahlia had made the newspapers was that reporters arrived at about the same time the cops did and it was on a public lot. These other murders, just as gruesome but very private, would never make it to the front pages.

He went into such detail that for a while, I thought he was trying to drive me out of the private-eye business or at least to get me off this case. If he hadn't asked for my help, I would have been certain of it.

* * * *

"Was it important?" the girl at the answering service asked when I called for more messages.

"Yeah, it was important. I'd think you'd be home in bed by now."

"No, I came on early this morning. You have one more message, from a Mister Albert Fane. He says he wants to talk to you about a Laura Prendergast. He didn't leave a number and he didn't know if you were in the office on Saturday, but he said he would be at your office at four-thirty today. I know that things about your cases are real important to you so I figured you would either get to me or you wouldn't and–"

"I'll be there," I said. I had to cut her off or she would go on forever.

Fane was Laura's name when she was a starlet, and I wondered if this was a former husband I didn't know about. I looked at my watch and saw that it was already after four.

I thanked her, hung up, and drove over to my office. There was a Saturday Matinee at the Palladium so my own lot was full. Teenagers didn't seem to give a damn that there was a sign that said, *For Occupants and Customers Only*. I found a parking spot down on Melrose and trotted back, hoping to catch Albert Fane.

On my way up the stairs, I saw a little guy in a dark suit standing outside my door with a hat in his hand. The hat was a bowler and the guy was Prendergast's butler.

"Mister Page? I'm so glad I caught you."

"What are you doing here?"

"I told your answering service that–"

"Albert?"

"Yes, sir."

I wouldn't ask about Saturday night until I heard what he had to tell me.

CHAPTER XXI

Prendergast's Butler fingered his bowler hat and he looked curiously around my office. When I gestured to the client chair, he looked at it with disgust, dusted it with his handkerchief and made an ugly face, but he did sit.

"I can hang your hat for you."

"No, thank you," he said.

I sat and waited.

"I ... I was wondering how you, uh, how you are doing in finding Laura's killer."

"We're getting someplace."

"We?"

"I have a partner," I said. No sense letting him pass on to Prendergast that the LAPD was really working the case.

"I see."

He bit into his lips and looked around some more. With him living in Prendergast's mansion, I didn't suppose he was used to being in a place that hadn't been painted since before the war.

"I'm not here on behalf of my employer but on behalf of myself."

I waited. When people come to a private detective, they sometimes have trouble getting out their words and even more trouble getting out their meaning.

"I saw Laura on Saturday night... I was with her at the Roosevelt Hotel. We took a taxi."

Anger was welling up inside me. It was all I could do to keep from screaming at him, but I forced myself to stay calm. "Tell the story, Mister Fane."

"Albert, please?"

"Albert then, yes." *Tell the damn story.*

"Yes, sir, of course. I don't mean to be so ... so reticent, but it is very difficult for me. You see, I was trying to bring her back to Mister Prendergast, and she agreed to come. Yes, she agreed. There was a taxi standing out front and I asked the driver to take me to Benedict Canyon.

He said that he would, but he drove a very short distance and he insisted that I get out."

Albert nodded.

"Yes, that was at Laurel Canyon Boulevard I think. Yes, I don't know the streets very well, but I do think that was it. I asked Laura to come with me and she said the she would, but not immediately. She said that she was not ready to go back to Mister Prendergast yet. I told her that she had promised, and she said she was sorry, but Mister Page, Laura has a history of breaking promises, not only to me, but to everyone.

He was talking almost too fast now, but I was not going to do anything to slow him down.

"I don't think the girl has ever kept – she never kept a promise in her life. I did everything I could for her. As a little girl, I treated her and her mother very well. When she was a young girl, a teenager, I suppose you would call it, she was very spoiled–"

He was confusing me. "I even arranged with my employer at the time to get her in as an extra at the MGM Studios. She was every grateful for that and she even started to give us Christmas presents and birthday presents. She helped me take care of her mother and she seemed very happy until she was let go at the studio."

He actually ran out of breath. He stopped for a big intake that ended in a deep sigh. While he tried to get his thoughts together, my thoughts were flying and I could not hold back the question that needed a definite answer.

"Are you Laura's father?"

"I thought I made that clear."

"I just wanted to be sure."

His eyes filled with tears and I felt like a ghoul for even asking.

"Yes, sir. I am her father," he said. "She was a headstrong girl, a lovely girl, as lovely as her mother when she was that age. Her mother's no longer alive. She would have been pleased at the marriage. But Mister Prendergast, he's so ... he feels so empty since the war. During the war, people from Washington came to see him, beautiful women fell at his feet."

"When did you start working for him?"

"In 1940, when he still had his house on Sunset Boulevard. He was well off then, but he was not rich. Well, not as rich as he is now. I was the first butler he ever had. He – but I'm getting off my purpose for being here. Mister Prendergast loved her very much. He was so afraid to lose her that he watched her every movement and–"

He stopped himself dead and tears were rolling down his cheeks and he brushed them away with a clean handkerchief.

"He loved her so much ... but because of what she was, what she became after she was no longer in the movies, he was afraid that anytime she was away that she was going to another man. And I'm afraid, sir, I'm afraid that it was sometimes true. There was something about her that demanded attention from men and one man did not seem to be enough."

He looked down at the bowler that he held in his lap. Then he looked up.

"Mister Prendergast never threatened her or went after her. He always forgave her when she came back. And she was never gone for more than a few hours at a time. Well, maybe overnight occasionally, but this last time, this time, she was gone for three days before we called you."

"We?"

"Yes. It was at my suggestion. He was afraid to report her to missing persons for fear that the publicity would damage her reputation. You see, Mister Page, Mister Prendergast thought that once she married him that everything about her past would be erased from the rolls of dishonor. He had forgiven everything. He forgave everything each time and he expected the world to be as forgiving as he was. He turned the other cheek so to speak, and she constantly disappointed him."

I remained silent, waiting for him to start up again, and when it didn't seem that it would happen, I asked a question. "What did the cab driver look like?"

"Handsome but rough, an attractive man. I had the feeling that she had him as a driver at sometime in the past, or that she knew him in some other way. No words passed between them, perhaps some looks. He seemed to know, as I did, that although she was leaving with me she was not entirely happy about it."

Albert was speeding up again.

"She was not afraid of Mister Prendergast. She treated him worse than he treated her. She was always shouting at him the way she had shouted at her mother and me when she was a girl. She said she wanted a divorce and that if he did not give it to her that–"

He stopped and shook his head. He was out of breath again.

"Nothing," he said.

"That's the one I want to hear."

"Yes, sir. She said she that she would have him murdered."

With all that, he had told me before that was the one that took gas out of me. I slumped in my chair. "Did she mean it?"

"I didn't hear it, but he told me, and it was quite clear that he believed her."

"When was that?"

"Two weeks ago. Just before, just before she disappeared."

"How did she go about disappearing?"

"Unbeknownst to Mister Prendergast, she called for a taxi and the taxi met her at the gate."

"Do you remember the name of the cab company?"

"I didn't see it. I was occupied elsewhere in the house. It was the last any of us saw of her until Saturday."

"How did you know where to find her?"

He closed his eyes and tears squeezed through. Then he took a breath. "She called me last Saturday. She knew it was usually my evening off. She asked me to meet her at the Roosevelt Hotel, and I did, and I tried to take her home, and, and that's why I am here today. I hoped you'd be here, but if not, I would have called on you at another time."

"How did you get here?" I expected him to say that he came by taxi, but he surprised me.

"Mister Prendergast loaned me one of his cars."

"*Why* are you here?"

"To plead for Mister Prendergast. He has the impression that neither you nor the police are doing anything to find Laura's killer. He thinks you may be just milking him and—"

"Assure him that I'm not. Did you have a car on Saturday night?"

"Yes, sir, but I did not try to take her home in it. I was afraid she would jump out. I thought that if I were sitting with her in the back seat of a taxicab she would not likely try to get away. And if she did, I could grab her and keep her from doing it. I didn't think in a million years that the driver would throw me out of his taxi. You see, Laura was so intuitive, especially with men, or perhaps she knew the driver and—"

"Knew him?"

"Just the looks that went between them. Or maybe they were just flirting. She always did flirt. She was good at it."

"So what happened after they threw you out of the car?"

He shrugged. "I was lost. I didn't know where I was, but after a while another taxi came along and I had him take me to Mister Prendergast's car."

"You went home?"

"What else could I do?"

Yeah, what else? "Why did she choose Prendergast as a husband?"

The question locked his face in an expression that I can't explain. Then it went through contortions of emotion: surprise, confusion, even happiness but finally, misery.

"I don't understand how, but I, I think Mister Prendergast bought her from some one."

"Bought her?" I wanted to hear it from him.

"I think you need a broader explanation. You see after she left motion pictures, she went to work as a ... as a..."

"Call girl?"

I thought he was going to break into sobs, but he quickly recovered, took a breath and said, "I suppose that is as gently as you can put it."

"Do you know who she went to work for?"

"No, sir. I know nothing of that kind of that life. But under it all she was ... she was..." He wanted to say she was a good girl, but I don't think he believed it.

"She was your daughter," I said.

"Yes."

"Does the name Michael Cameron mean anything to you? Or Salvatore Trugante?"

"No, sir. Neither name." It had been a long time since I had seen a man is such agony just talking. "I so do not want it to be Mister Prendergast who goes to jail. He was nothing but good for her."

"Even if he's the one who—"

"He couldn't have. Not in a million years."

Was that Albert Fane's ploy? Was he here to try to clear Prendergast, or was he trying to get me to suspect Prendergast? At the mansion, his expression was impassive, but I had watched his face for the last twenty minutes, and I was trying to read his thoughts. His tears were real, his quivering, his shaking, his sobbing, all of it was real.

"Since Mister Prendergast has hired me to try to find Laura's killer, why would I believe it was him?" I asked.

"You almost said it."

"You tell me."

"Because he is so strange and so alone. Laura was the first good thing that happened to him since he sold his aircraft plants."

He was doing and saying the right things, but I needed more. "Are you aware that the police are looking for a little man in a bowler hat who left the Roosevelt Hotel with your daughter on Saturday night?"

His eyes widened.

I threw another one at him. "What do you know about Misty Crest Road?"

He seemed puzzled. "I used to own a house there."

"Used to?"

"My wife took the house in the divorce settlement. She died just last year."

"And the house?"

"I suppose it's still in her estate. I think Laura inherited it. It was probably destined for her."

Destined was a good word. Maybe *doomed* was better.

"What was your wife's name?" I asked. It was something that Sandiri could check in five minutes if he didn't already know. He gave me the name Loretta.

"I'm afraid, Mister Fane, Albert, that I don't buy your story."

"It's the only story I have," he said. "I'll pay you to find the killer if Mister Prendergast doesn't."

"Does he know that Laura was your daughter?"

"Yes, sir, but he never holds it over me. Or over her for that matter." He had wiped his eyes, but they were as full again.

"Did he know she was your daughter before he married her?"

His "No" just hung there. It was neither truth nor lie, but something in between. "What can I pay you as an advance?" he asked.

"Nothing. I'm still working for Prendergast."

I stood and he looked up at me.

"I could contribute," he said.

"No thank you," I said.

He could not believe that I was dismissing him. He had come here as much to talk it out or to mislead me as to give me information or to hire me. If I let him, he would stay until it was time for him to go back on duty as Tyree Prendergast's butler.

As far as I was concerned, Albert Fane was still a suspect. I would not give his name to Sandiri yet, but I would pass on the information that Albert had given me.

* * * *

I called Sandiri and expected him to be surprised to learn that I knew who owned the house on Misty Crest. Instead, he surprised me.

"I already got that. It was Laura Fane's house," he said. "She just inherited it from her mother."

"What about her father?"

"Don't know anything about him yet, just that he divorced the mother a few years back."

"Why?"

"What do you want to know for?"

"Just curious."

"Cruelty," he said.

"Albert? Cruel?"

"No, she was cruel to him."

CHAPTER XXII

"Early to bed and early to rise makes a man healthy, wealthy and wise."

I think Ben Franklin said that, but sometimes early to bed just means that I need more sleep – especially when I can't stay awake on a Saturday night.

I was counting money when somebody banged at my door.

"Wait a minute," I called.

I was getting awfully close to ten thousand dollars and I wanted to get it into the bank before they closed. The banging was insistent and so was the female voice.

"Let me in," she said.

Not by the hair of my chinny, chin, chin. Hell, it was only a dream anyhow.

I forced myself awake, swung my legs from the bed and grabbed my terry cloth robe from the back of a chair. I had it most of the way on before I asked who was on the other side of the door.

"Alice," she said. All that banging and yelling and now she was whispering. But a private eye doesn't ask too many questions when a client's daughter wants to get in – especially when the client is Salvatore Trugante.

I opened the door and she hurried into the apartment looking at the walls and taking five strides through to the kitchen. She checked the bedroom and the bathroom too. Her blonde hair was coiled in the back and fixed in place with combs. She wore high heels and something that looked like a party dress. It was yellow and cinched tight. She was showing bare shoulders, but not much of a pregnant belly.

"God, this is a cracker box," she said and she sat on the overstuffed sofa against one wall. "Ouch! These springs will cut right through you!"

"Did I make fun of your swimming pool? What are you doing here?"

"Somebody's after me," she said. She didn't seem scared enough.

"Like who?"

"How do I know who? I was sitting in Chelsea when these two goons came in. One of them spots me and starts to come in my direction."

Chelsea was a bar near the Yucca.

"I didn't like the looks of them, so I got up to leave," she said. "But it was like they started to surround me. One was coming around one side of the room and one around the other, but the dummies, they don't leave anybody at the door and I walked straight that way. Thank God there was a cab at the curb."

"What kind of cab?"

"What difference does it make?"

"Probably none, but humor me."

"I don't remember, but I remembered that you lived in the neighborhood, so here I am."

"Why didn't you have the cab take you home?"

"Because I had it bring me here." It was an answer I'd have to live with. I went to make sure I had locked the door.

"Did they follow you?"

"Not as far as I know." She glanced the length of my terry cloth robe. "You going swimming?"

"Silk robes are for gentleman. You're lucky I didn't answer in the buff."

"Lucky, huh? Some gentleman you are. The least you could do is offer me a drink."

"It's the middle of the night."

"It's only eleven-thirty."

I looked into the kitchen and saw that the chef clock hanging against the wall had his short hand up and his long hand pointing to his crotch.

"I'll take you home," I said.

"No."

"What you mean, 'no?'"

"I mean I don't want to go home."

"Then I'll call your father and tell him to come get you."

"You bastard!" Women keep calling me that.

I grabbed the phone from the full-size teacher's desk that I picked up at an auction when the city was closing down one of the old schools.

Alice rose from the sofa and put her finger on the cradle before I could get though to an operator. She stood very close to me, looking up with her very big and very brown eyes. Her perfume was too strong for such a young woman, too strong for any woman as a matter of fact, but something about it sent a message to the more interested parts of my anatomy.

"My stomach's still almost flat," she said.

"It won't be flat very long and I'm way too old for you."

"You didn't say that last year when you bought me an illegal drink."

She was right. Last year she wasn't twenty yet, but I was horny as hell, and my morality gets pretty flexible when that happens. I didn't know she was Sal Trugante's daughter then either, but now I did. Forbidden fruit gets pretty enticing. The knowledge of potential consequences did not quell my excitement until my brain took over.

At least, it was trying to take over.

She was looking at me while wearing a little grin. It would be so easy to bring my mouth to hers and to plant a long and lingering kiss. She was small and she would be easy to carry to my bed, easy to undress, easy to–

"I'll take you home," I said. It was my brain talking.

She went up on her toes, but even in high heels, my mouth was too far for her reach. She nibbled with her lips at my neck.

"We had fun together, didn't we," she whispered.

Yes, for a few weeks we did. She was a screamer, one of the first screamers I ran into on this side of the Atlantic, but many women were doing it now. Word must've gotten out that men liked it. Or maybe it was something that came back from Paris as rumor and it was beginning to catch on – like all the other stuff. Maybe that was why the roaring twenties were so hot, because men had come back from Paris. The whole sex thing must have skipped a generation, or maybe it was because they were so long without legal booze.

She was pressing against the front of me. Her breasts were just over my belly and she was letting me see the cleft. I hunched my back and brought my mouth to hers. She began to explore my lips with her tongue. She seemed to have forgotten about the men who had surrounded her in the Chelsea, but I hadn't.

I gripped her upper arms and moved her away. She was smirking and that made her all the more enticing. Yes, forbidden fruit, the daughter of Salvatore Trugante, and as sexy as they come in small packages. I took a step toward her and I stopped.

"I'd better get you home."

"If you don't make love to me, I'll tell Papa that you did."

"And I'll tell him that I didn't. I think he knows you well enough to know who the liar is."

Her expression went from temptress to spoiled brat. She moved both hands to her dress at the left side of her body, and I thought she was going for a gun she had hidden. Before I could grab her, she had grabbed the material of her party dress with both hands and ripped it, revealing a wire corset thing that was holding her breasts. I gripped her hands with my own, so she couldn't tear the corset. Any pressure I used to pull her hands away might tear the corset down the front.

Her eyes were sparkling and she smiled.

For just a second, I thought I might just as well die for the truth as for a lie, but I released her hands. She showed her teeth and ripped away the corset exposing her smallish, uptipped breasts.

I planted my mouth on hers hard, and the sash of my robe came loose. I lifted her and carried her to the sofa she had complained about. I reached for the corset to tear it the rest of the way, but as soon as my fingers hit her flesh, I drew back as if I had touched fire.

"Fuck me, you bastard. I can see you're interested."

I closed my robe, knotted the sash and backed away. "Get dressed. I'll call for a cab."

"I won't leave until morning."

"Then don't," I said. I went into the bedroom and latched the door from inside.

In a few minutes, she tried to get in.

"Bastard," she said. There was that word again.

I didn't get much sleep because I kept thinking of her in my living room. I wondered what she was doing, or if she had gone home.

In the middle of the night, I got up to go to the bathroom. In the faint light that filtered through the kitchen, I saw her lying asleep on the sofa under my trench coat. One of the sofa cushions was on the floor, the one with the busted spring, and she was snoring away.

* * * *

Late the next morning, she was more reasonable. We agreed on a story that would explain the torn dress. "Papa would kill you if he thought you raped me."

"No kidding."

As I drove her back to her father's house high over Laurel Canyon, I asked her about Merriman, and she said nothing. A few minutes later, I asked her again.

"He's a mama's boy with no mama," she said. I asked her what that meant. She explained that Normie Merriman liked his women older and tougher than she was.

"They don't come much tougher than you are," I said.

"If that's supposed to be a compliment, thanks, but when are we going to really do something?"

"About what?"

"About me wanting to get laid."

"At your wedding night, I suppose."

"I am *not* getting married."

"You'll find somebody."

"You sound like one of my aunts. They're looking for somebody too. I really did have fun with you, and those two bodybuilders weren't all that good at making me happy."

If she was working up to a proposal, I was making it a point not to hear it.

"So that's where we leave it?" she finally asked.

"Yes."

Instead of getting angry, she sulked.

When we turned onto Laurel Canyon Boulevard, I asked her what she thought of Michael Cameron.

"He's all right."

"Know him pretty well?"

"Used to."

"How well?"

"I don't talk about it."

"Why?"

"Because he's a bastard who sells women."

"You liked him a lot, huh?"

"Will you shut up?"

We passed the torpedo at the gate and I was making my first turn onto the zigzag road that led to her father's house.

"What if I tell Papa that you raped me?" she said.

"I'll have to take my chances, but once I'm dead, we're finished." I sounded far more confident than I felt.

"Should I tell him it was Normie?"

"Tell him whatever you like. Was it?"

"Could've been. Could've been a lot of guys. Do you think Papa would kill him?"

"No."

"Papa was pretty mad when I told him I was pregnant."

"My bet is that he wasn't surprised that you were screwing, just that you got pregnant. I think he figured you for smarter."

"Ooo, you are a bastard. I'm not going to tell him who it was, and nobody will know until they give a half dozen guys blood tests."

"Did it happen when you got raped at Santa Monica?"

Her chin snapped in my direction. "How did you know about that?"

"Is that when it was?"

"Yes."

"Was it really rape? Or was it more like you tried to work with me last night? An experience you wanted to learn first hand?"

She looked down at her fingernails as we started up the winding road toward the top of the hill. She was almost crying.

"Are you going to tell Papa about that?" she asked.

"Not unless I have to."

"Is that a threat?"

"That wasn't what I meant," I said, but I guess in a sense it was.

"I'm going to stick to the story we talked about," she said.

"Do you have any idea who the guys were who came after you last night?"

"Thugs."

"No shit."

"Is that sarcasm?"

I didn't reply.

"Probably some of Papa's rivals," she said.

"Did you recognize them?"

"Bugsy Siegel's guys maybe. Papa can't compete with them. They have stronger connections."

"I thought Bugsy was putting all of his efforts into that night club in Las Vegas."

"I hope this doesn't start a war." She opened the trench coat I had loaned her to show the torn dress and corset.

"Tell him they did it. If he thinks he can't compete, he's not likely to retaliate."

"You don't know Papa. He gets mad and... You know, he could use somebody like you."

"No thanks."

"Maybe even as a son-in-law."

I steered the Ford a little too sharply at the last turn, and I saw her smirk.

"Just stick to the story," I said.

CHAPTER XXIII

When I stopped in front of the house, I noticed that Dixie's Pontiac was back in the garage area. I thought it strange for a Sunday.

"We have to see Papa," Alice said, but the silver suit on the front door patted me down anyway. I had left my .45 at home.

We waited in his office like it was the middle of the week instead of Sunday afternoon. Dixie wasn't at her desk, but it did not take long for Trugante to come down. Instead of a suit, he was wearing in a red silk robe with red silk pajama legs and leather slippers showing below the hem. I guess even old Italian gentlemen played *bon vivant* every now and then. I wondered if he got the robe the same place Cameron got the smoking jacket.

Alice threw her arms around his neck and started spitting out her story the moment he stepped into the room. She told it in rapid-fire fashion beginning with how two men had chased her from the Chelsea and down a dark alley where they had started to rip her clothes off and that I had rescued her

She explained that the reason she did not come home was that she was embarrassed. She went on to tell him what an absolute gentleman I was. She said that I let her sleep in my bed while I slept on an awful sofa. The last part was a shot at my lack of chivalry.

A lot of what she said was what we agreed on. Some of it she embellished. I made it a point to remember the details in case I was cross-examined by Sal or one of his thugs.

"So Page, did you recognize these men?"

"Typical thugs, not Italian though."

I almost bit my tongue. What I meant to say was that I didn't think they had anything to do with his mob.

"If they weren't my men, whose men were they?" I was surprised that he understood what I meant.

"I have no idea. As soon as they heard me coming, they were gone."

"That's not true, Papa. He hit one of them and busted his nose."

Trugante raised his brow.

"Poetic license," I said.

He grinned, but she didn't know what that meant.

"Thanks," he said, but I don't think he knew what it meant either. "You got anything on that other?"

"I'll be ready to give you a report tomorrow or the next day."

"Little girl, you're going to make your papa and old man before his time."

"Thank you, Rick." She went up on her toes and I allowed her to peck me lightly on the lips.

She grinned at her father and hurried away to the elevator.

He squinted at me. "She ask you to marry her?"

"Huh?"

"Just kidding," he said, and he patted me on the cheek. "You English, you don't understand humor."

* * * *

Unless they had changed shifts, I figured I would get a different dispatcher at the Wilshire Cab Company than the one who had showed me the phony log from cab number 729. I wasn't going to ask for that log again, but I did have some other questions.

The guy who works on Sunday afternoon was older than silent movies. He had gray hair, but his skin color was good and he had a big belly.

"Do you lease cabs to regular customers?" I said.

"What d'ya mean?" He looked hard at me.

"If I want a cab to pick me up at the same time every morning can you–"

"Yeah, we can arrange that. Where you want to be picked up?"

"Hold on a minute. I'm trying to find out a few things."

"What things?"

"Is it all right for me to ask a few questions?"

"Yeah. We love that kind of business. If you're gonna be long, sit in the chair there. I don't like people looking down at me. Where I know you from?"

"I don't think you do."

"Maybe not. Speak up. What d'ya want to know?"

"Do you have radios in your cabs?"

"Not so far. The boss is thinking about getting them though. He says it'll improve business. You ask me, we'll get a lot of bullshit calls and when we get there for the pickup, people across the street will be laughing their asses off. You know, like kids calling a tobacco store and asking if they got Prince Albert in a can? 'Yeah.' 'Well, let him out.' Kids! They think they're funny, especially those Beverly Hills brats. What else d'ya wanna know?"

"Do you have satisfied customers so that–"

"All our customers are satisfied. What d'ya think? We dump people off at the wrong place and all that bullshit?" He was a wonderful spokesman for his company.

"No, I mean do you have some names so I can–"

"Got a pencil?" He pulled open the top right drawer, pulled out a clipboard and folded up the fake leather cover. He started to read and I started to write names and telephone numbers.

The third one was Patricia Drake. "She gets a ride from her house in Beverly Hills every Monday morning, gets a ride back every Friday." He gave the phone number and both of the addresses. The place she went on Monday was where she decked me with the frying pan. I figured she'd be avoiding that one for Normie's sake.

He reeled off two more names and asked me if that was enough. "Keep going," I said. I was tempted to throw out a fiver, but that would have stopped him dead, so I just kept writing. After six names, I thought it was a good idea to stop. If he wasn't suspicious now, he should be.

"Will I always get the same driver?"

"Usually."

"Does Mister Cameron have that kind of arrangement?" I asked him.

"How'd you know about him?"

"He's the one who referred me."

"Hell, if the boss referred you, why're you asking all these questions? Mister Michael gets any kind of arrangement he wants."

"How long's he owned this place?"

"Just about a year now. Who did you say you were?" He tilted his head away and squinted with one eye.

"One of his other customers," I said.

"What other customers?"

"Oh, jeez, I'm sorry. I–" I pretended to stammer through an apology saying without saying that I knew what Cameron's other business was.

"Why you checking? If you're satisfied the other way?" the guy said.

"Just careful, I suppose. Can you have one of your people pick me up at this address tomorrow morning at four a.m.?"

"Four in the morning?"

"Yeah."

"Okay. You want me to put you down for every morning at four?"

"Just tomorrow will be fine for the time being."

"My guy'll be there at four on the button. You just be ready. What's your name again?"

I gave him one of the many phony business cards that I had printed up for "Richard Grange." It gave the address and phone number of a real estate office in my building as well as my true home address. I had a deal with the real estate guy that any calls for Richard Grange would be referred to me.

I left my car on the office lot and walked back to my apartment where the cabbie would pick me up in the morning.

I lay in the dark listening to Fred Allen's weekly radio trip down Allen's Alley. After that, I faded to sleep. I got up around midnight and flicked off the radio. It seemed like no time at all before my clock was clanging that it was three-thirty in the a.m.

The cabbie knocked at four a.m. and ten seconds, according to the belly of the chef on my kitchen wall. On the way into the cab, I checked the number on the door. It was not the infamous "729."

"Awful about that cabbie getting shot last week," I said.

"He was practically the boss's chauffeur," the driver was blonde and old enough to have been in the war.

"Who got that job?"

"Some goon."

"Goon?"

"You know the type, don't know right from left. Thinks the world is his. Doesn't even have a hack license, but they get around it somehow... How come you go to the real estate business so early in the morning?"

"I'm expecting a client who wants to run up to Santa Barbara to see a house."

"You guys travel like that?"

"Good money in it."

"Glad there's good money in something."

I watched out of the cab as the night passed by. When I came back from Europe, I saw how much L.A. had grown during the war and it had grown even more during the year I was back. "Go west, young man," someone said a long, long time ago. I was not sure how many people took his advice then, but they damn sure were taking it now.

"How many regular clients do you have?" I asked.

"Two or three others. Got this good-looking blonde I bring down from Beverly Hills. I take her over to Santa Monica every week."

"Movie star?"

"Could've been. Don't remember."

"Ever talk to her?"

"She talks some. Nice lady. She's my last fare today."

"All the way to Santa Monica, huh?"

"Yep."

"Ever pick up fares along the way?"

"If somebody's going the same way."

"If it doesn't work out with this guy going to Santa Barbara, what do you say you pick me up at the office here and ride me out there."

"With the lady?"

"Put me in the front seat. What time do you pick her up?"

"What's this about?"

"Research."

He squinted at me, then shrugged. "I pick her up at noon on the top."

"Grab me here at eleven-thirty," I said.

He pulled the cab to the curb in front of my building. I paid him and gave him a five-dollar tip just to make certain he would come back at noon.

"How do you know Santa Barbara ain't gonna work out?"

"Sometimes you get a feeling about a guy. You know, like you get a feeling about a fare?"

"Yeah, I know what you mean – you want to go to Santa Monica with the lady so you can do some research." He smiled and he flicked the flag on his meter.

When I went into my office, I realized that someone had been there. They had used the ashtray, but they had dumped the ashes in the clean can, and my desk calendar was in a different place. My middle desk drawer was locked, but locking it was something I never did. Someone had used a skeleton key.

I went to the side drawer and looked at the file marked *Trugante* and the other marked *Prendergast*. Both had been put in exact alphabetical order. My use of the alphabet was approximate. Five T files and three P files with the most current file in the front of that part of the alphabet. Whoever it was had put the other P and T files in exact order as well. There was nothing in either file because I kept the important paperwork of ongoing cases at my desk at the apartment. On nights when I couldn't sleep, I sometimes got up and shuffled papers.

I would check with Sandiri later to see if he had been in, but I didn't think so.

I walked over to the Yucca Café that was just opening. It was closer to my apartment than my office, but I wanted the "special run" in the cab.

CHAPTER XXIV

Miss Kathryn was a good-looking brunette with breasts that put Dixie to shame. She was working behind the bar while others were cooking and waiting on tables. I remembered seeing her here before, but not very often.

"Morning," I said.

"It sure is. What can I get you?"

"Eggs over easy with crisp bacon and toast."

"On the way," she said, and she called it across the pass-through. "Coffee?"

"Do people drink booze this early?" I asked.

"We don't serve alcohol till eleven. It keeps the drunks out. Mostly we get movie people who're getting ready for the grind. Are you the fellow that Trevor said wanted to talk to me?"

"Probably." I didn't remember telling Trevor that, but I had asked questions about her. Everybody is a detective of sorts.

"He says you wanted to know about Alice Smith."

"I'm working for her father."

"Which means I can't tell you anything."

She smiled and walked over to the next customer. While she was gone, I worked on my appeal.

When she came back, I explained. "You wouldn't want a baby to go without a daddy would you?"

She frowned.

"Bacon crisp and eggs easy," the short order guy yelled from the pass-through. Miss Kathryn put them on the bar in front of me. It was odd even thinking of her as "Miss Kathryn," because she was younger than I was, but that was what Trevor had called her so it stuck in my head.

"Let me think about it," she said.

She left from behind the bar to bus two of the tables. When she came back, she asked what I wanted to know.

"The names of anybody who might have been friends with her in the last couple of months?"

"Define 'couple of months?'" She made a good point.

"Three months?"

"Still thinking," she said, and she walked back into the kitchen, maybe even to her office.

She was friendly and smart. I had the feeling that she was sizing me up for whatever kind of bastard I might be. The only bastard I was, as far as I knew, was that I was a private detective. We stick our noses a lot of places where they don't seem to belong, and I might stick mine in places that other Sherlocks won't go. It's probably the reason that I always have a job.

I had dabbed what wet yolk was left with the toast, and I was cutting into the egg with my fork when she came back.

"You know that what I tell you is confidential. And if it comes back to me, in any way, shape, or form, I'll poison you the next time you're in."

"Fair enough."

"Alice – and I know damn well her name's not Smith – spreads herself pretty thick. Mostly she's in at night, so Trevor knows about that, but the way I figure it, early in the morning is when it's serious."

I did not necessarily agree with her, but I nodded.

"Last three months? Two different guys: a good-looking kid who looks like he belongs on the beach and he probably does. The other guy is older, also good-looking, looks like he's got a lot of money. I heard her call him 'Michael.' The blonde kid is named 'Norman' or 'Normie.' I hope that helps because that's all I have. How are the eggs?"

"Perfect," I said.

For her, I over-tipped enormously, but something told me she would pass it on to the hired help.

* * * *

I keep many hats in the closet in the office: a spare fedora, a baseball cap, a construction worker's hard hat, a navy pea cap, an army officer's cap and an enlisted man's cap. I had no taxi driver's cap so I asked the driver if I could borrow his. I gave him twenty bucks and explained why I needed it.

"Just as long as you don't bring me into it," he said. He slid over to the passenger side.

When we reached Patty Drake's place, he held the door for her and introduced me as a driver he had in training. The cap came down to bend my ears and I thrust out my lower lip. I was trying to look like Edgar Bergen's other dummy, Mortimer Snerd.

Patty Drake said "Okay" and she chuckled. "Are you going to take over my ride?"

"No, ma'am. Just here for the trainin'." I let out a little laugh, but this time, I toned it down. I was trying to do Dixie Joy's accent, but I was coming off stupid.

"By the way, I want you to pick up somebody else for me," she said. "You don't mind do you, Jay?"

"No, ma'am," the cabbie said.

I watched her in the rearview mirror. She did not look like a woman who was planning to have a good time. Chances were good that she had misgivings about going back to Santa Monica, but what could she do? Normie was a surfer.

I thought it might be something else though, especially when we stopped at an apartment building off Lincoln Boulevard and she had to force a smile to greet young Norman.

He came from the building with a surfboard, one piece of luggage, and a towel tossed over his shoulder. Jay put the bag in the trunk of the taxi, but we had to thrust the surfboard on a diagonal from the left rear to the front right so that it cramped the hell out of my copilot.

At the next traffic signal, Jay said he would drive.

"Oh, you don't have to do that. You just sit here in the back with us," Patty Drake said. "Let your driver get his training." She was good-looking and sexy, but she was reaching that age where she was starting to sound like somebody's mother.

"Have you talked to Alice?" she said to Normie.

"She won't talk to me."

"Does her father know?"

"Her father don't know shit. As far as he's concerned–" Normie cut himself off.

I didn't learn anything else until Patty directed me to a motel, still in Santa Monica but closer to North Beach.

The place we left them at was a beachfront motel with sliding doors that faced the water. It was three hundred yards from the place where she had banged me over the head with the frying pan, but they must have figured it was safe.

"Changing your resort?" Jay said.

"Better waves," Normie said.

Good surfing waves were something I wouldn't know about, but it was a better excuse for changing locations than saying they had an embarrassing situation at the other place.

"Should I pick you up here on Friday?" Jay asked Patty Drake.

"This is where we'll be," she said.

I helped with the bags and the surfboard and took them up the outside stairs to a second floor apartment on the end. Patty tipped me a dollar. I gave it to Jay when I went back to the cab.

"Learn what you needed?" Jay said.

"Not everything," I said.

We were only at Ocean Park Boulevard when I pulled to the side and gave him his hat back.

"What's the matter?"

"I'm tired of driving. Is she always with the same guy?"

"This is the first time I had to pick him up, but I've seen him before. He's usually waiting for her... Did the Malibu real estate thing fall through?"

"I told you I didn't trust the guy."

"Not good to trust people," he said. He gave me a dismissive wave. Then he said, "You're working for Mister Cameron, aren't you?"

The smart thing might be to say yes, but I repeated the partial truth, that I was a private detective checking on the woman, and he seemed to buy it. He seemed too clean cut to be on the inside of a Cameron enterprise. I asked him what he did besides drive a cab. He said he was going to Southern Cal on the G.I. Bill.

When he brought me back to my office, I gave him another twenty. "That's to keep this whole thing quiet."

"You got it. And if you need me tomorrow morning at–"

"Probably not, but if I do, I'll ask for you."

"Thanks," he said. He was delighted at the extra cash that I would be charging to Trugante. I hoped that Trugante understood expenses.

* * * *

I went back to my office to check my mail and my messages. Dixie left a message for me to call her tonight. "And a girl named Alice called, but she wouldn't leave a number. Mister Trugante says you are to call him immediately," the girl at the answering service said.

I called Trugante.

"Rick Page," Trugante said, as if it was the first time we had ever spoken.

"Yes, sir?"

"I want you in my office in ten minutes."

It was impossible to get to his office in ten minutes, but he made the urgency clear, and I arrived in less than twenty minutes.

Dixie rolled her eyes when she saw me, and tilted her head toward the office. "He says you should go right in."

I thought it was a good sign that Trugante was pacing.

"Page, what am I paying you for?"

"To find the father to your grandchild." That one was easy enough.

"Am I paying you to fuck my daughter?"

"No, sir, you're not and I'm not doing that."

"She says–"

"That she slept in my bed, and that's a lie. I made her sleep on the couch."

"You made my daughter do what?"

"I had to lock myself in my room."

"She says that you brought her up to your room, gave her a couple of drinks, ripped her clothes off, and fucked her."

"I brought her to my apartment, she didn't need a couple of drinks, she tried to–"

He put up his hand. "I don't want to hear it!"

So, I didn't say it.

"How old are you, Page?"

I was afraid of where he might be going with that one.

"Thirty-two," I said.

"And she's twenty?"

"Mister Trugante, I–"

"You should be old enough to know what goes on with a girl like that. She spreads herself around. She wants this one, she wants that one, she wants another one. You, I understand. Decent looking guy, smart as far as I can figure out, so she gives you bullshit about a guy after her that rips her dress off, and you fall for it. I understand it, but I don't like it."

"It didn't happen, Mister Trugante," I said. I told him the whole story as I remembered it. For the few facts that I recited, he interrupted me about half a dozen times.

"A bullshit story she tells you too, huh?" he says.

"No, I think that part may have been true."

"But you ripped her dress?"

"She ripped her own dress."

"If she was a man..." He huffed and sat behind his desk. "A son instead of a daughter..." He looked at the ceiling and put up both hands as if he were surrendering.

I understood what he was trying to say. He was from a generation when women did not screw out of marriage – not publicly anyhow. The only women who were supposed to enjoy sex were his wife, his girl friends, or well-chosen prostitutes. I made an assumption about his wife because he was Italian and most Italian girls I had been with liked making love. There were those words again, "making love."

"I gotta find that girl a husband. You gotta tell me you're close to finding him."

"Very close."

"You been looking for a week now."

"Yes, sir."

"So what do you have?" He changed the subject so quickly that I knew he never believed Alice's story from the first word. He wanted a report that I told him I would not give him yet, but I threw him some scraps.

"I've narrowed it down to two people. I'll have something more concrete tomorrow or the next day," I said. But I also thought I might be zeroing in on a killer. Another trip to Santa Monica might tell me that. I would be on my way to check on it already if he hadn't called me in.

"For sure tomorrow?"

"Or the next day."

"My grand-baby ain't getting any younger," he said.

"I understand. You'll have a son-in-law by the weekend."

"Do you think it should be a big wedding?"

I didn't think he was really asking me, but I tailored a reply to comfort him. "She'll get pregnant on her wedding night," I said.

He seemed almost pleased. Then he leveled his gaze. "If you don't come up with a father by tomorrow, you're gonna need to get a tuxedo."

He was serious.

On my way out of his office, Dixie slipped me a note. I read it when I got back into my car. *Why haven't you called? I'll be at the motel by six*, the note read.

Santa Monica was my next stop. I did not think I would be back by six.

CHAPTER XV

How those guys who sat on surfboards went out in the winter was something that I would never understand, but they were out there. I assumed that Normie Merriman was one of them. I knocked on the door of the apartment.

"Yes?" Patty Drake said.

"They said you needed some extra towels," I said.

"I didn't call for ... well, okay."

She opened the door, and as soon as she saw me, she tried to close it on me, but I muscled my way inside, first the shoulder, then the rest of me.

"I'll scream if you–"

"If you scream, I'll make sure you go to jail."

She was wearing a bathing suit. Maybe she planned to get some sun, even in the fifty-degree temperatures. All beach people were crazy, I thought.

"When are you going to tell him?" I asked her.

"Tell him what?"

"That you're finished with him."

She looked at me, her eyes misty. "You're making an assumption that you know nothing about."

"I do a lot of that. It's also one of the things I'm good at."

She looked away again and out over the water. I think I identified the one of four surfers as Normie Merriman, also known as Norman Merriman, Jr.

"I'm sure you were good for him while it lasted."

"And he was good for me."

"But all good things–"

"You don't have to say it."

"Is Cameron trying to draw you back in?"

"I'm doing some of that on my own, gathering a little money, thinking about going back to Upstate New York. He'll be out there for a while. For a hundred bucks–"

"Stop it," I said.

"Yeah."

I opened my wallet and put a hundred dollars on the chair near the sliding glass.

She looked down at the money then up at me. "You bastard."

"Not for that. For information."

She frowned.

"I'm going to tell you a bunch of things, and you're going to tell me where I'm wrong. You and Normie were at the Roosevelt Hotel the Saturday before last, right?"

"Wrong."

"Wrong?"

"I was there with his father."

"His father?"

"I know, he seems like a shit, but he's got something, just like Normie has something. And more than that, he has money."

"And a wife?"

"Dead long ago, but that's not going to do me any good."

"Why not?"

"Because I see what's going on."

"I don't understand."

"Cameron and Trugante were recruiting at the Roosevelt. Something's happening. More people are coming to L.A. More money is being made at the top, more men need to get laid, more women need to pay their bills. It's getting expensive to live out here."

"Why were you at the party?"

"Am I that bad?"

"No. You're damned attractive for a woman your age. You're telling people early thirties, but your closer to forty, right?"

She laughed. "I guess it does show."

"Not except for the maturity. Is he looking for a mother?"

Her mouth fell open.

"I don't mean in the literal sense."

She chuckled. "You're right. He's a smart boy, but he needs somebody to tell him what to do."

"What was his father doing at the Roosevelt?"

She looked up at me. "The same as everybody else, recruiting. Testing the goods, so to speak."

"With you there?"

"With me on his arm as kind of a confidence booster. He didn't think I knew that. You see, Mister Page, he's through with me. I'm too old for him. You know how men are."

"Have you been doing this for Trugante and Cameron for a long time?"

"For a very long time. It's been six years since I stopped working Michael's calls. I didn't want to swing over to the houses and I damn sure didn't want to be one of Michael's 'special girls.' I don't like him. I don't like listening to him. I don't like talking to him. I definitely don't like doing what he says."

"Like what?"

"There's a lot of stuff going on. Michael brings the good new girls up from Sal's houses, and the old stuff comes down from Michael."

"Who's the boss?"

"Trugante is the over-boss. Cameron does the calls. His dapper presence collects the clients. He even sends some of the outside referrals to Trugante's houses. He doesn't like it, but he does it."

"How did you get away with a recruiting party in a place like the Roosevelt?"

"Under the guise of an inventor's convention. We started on Friday, ended Sunday morning. We told the people at the hotel that it was very hush-hush, inside stuff. Very important to the movie industry. They shouldn't tell anyone. They were thrilled to do it and thrilled to have the business."

"So thrilled that they lied to the police?"

"I don't know what they did with the police. I just know what went on, and what the people at the hotel thought."

"Did you know Laura Fane?"

Her "Yes" barely escaped her throat.

"Do you know what happened to her?"

"Married that airplane fellow, right?" Something bothered her.

"I mean on Saturday night. You saw her Saturday, right? With a little guy with a bowler hat?"

She shrugged. "I asked her what she was doing and she told me to go to hell. She had nothing to do with the convention. She just happened to have a room there."

"Is that what she told you?"

"She said this old guy had come to rescue her."

"Rescue?"

"Take her back to her husband. She said she was finished with Cameron."

"Where was Trugante?"

"I'm not sure. Maybe that was when he was talking with Dixie Joy."

"Did you see Normie there?"

She laughed. "He came to try to pull me out of there, just like that old man was rescuing Laura. He was afraid I was going back into the business. His father saw him and started a scene. Michael reasoned with both of them, if you can call tossing Normie out on his ass 'reasoning.' Some of the hotel people got upset about that, but Michael, charmer that he is, smoothed it over for all of us, all of *them*. I was paid well for my night."

"Did you see Laura after Saturday night?"

"She went back to her husband."

I had to do a little acting to keep from telling her too much. "Could she have left with Normie?"

"Men his age are never satisfied. They need sex all the time. I couldn't go with him. Michael was paying me too well to recruit. Normie had had his eyes on Laura. On Dixie too and on two or three other girls. Laura was driving him crazy though. He saw something in her he didn't see in the rest of us. He wanted her too. I think he might even have tussled with her and the little old guy outside, but in the end, Laura left with the old guy."

"Where did they go?"

"They left in a taxi. That's all I know."

"Do you know anything about the old guy, the one with bowler hat?"

"Only that he wasn't registered in the hotel."

"Did you know the cab driver who took them was the one who was murdered last week?"

She closed her eyes. She knew.

"Did he ever drive you?"

"Only when I was working for Michael, but that was before the war. I think he was in the army for a while."

"Many of us were."

"He was more like Michael's chauffeur than just a taxi driver. He was always on call for Michael."

"How well does Michael know Alice Trugante?"

She chuckled. "He had to beat her off with a broom, and he was smart enough to do that."

"Smart enough?"

"Nobody wants Sal breathing down their necks."

"When's the last time Normie saw Alice?"

"A week? Two weeks? He sees her off and on. I don't know when the last time was, but he still likes her." She nodded toward the water. "He's coming up now."

I looked out to the ocean. He was in knee-deep water carrying his surfboard. Now was not the time to confront him. I left the hundred dollars, but I was not sure whose expenses I would mark it against.

"When are you going to tell him that you're through?"

"When I leave here on Friday. Earlier if I have to."

"You might have to," I said, but I didn't explain.

* * * *

I drove back to the place where we had picked up Normie this morning. I slipped the super a couple of bucks and he let me look at the room. There was not much there. He had a few things hanging in the closet, some underwear in the drawers, and an extra pair of shoes.

I opened his suitcase and found photographs, glamour shots of Dixie and Patty. A nude of Patty when she was younger, tastefully done, an "art" photo he would have called it. There was a piece of frayed clothesline rope, photos of him in the army, probably at Officer Candidate School. There were some of him with his surfboard. There were separate photos of him smiling at the camera with Dixie, Patty, Alice and the little redhead who worked for his father. There were also some photos of him with women I didn't recognize. I took the best of the photos of him and Alice and slipped it into my pocket.

Then I went through the photos again. There were none of him and Laura.

* * * *

It was almost seven o'clock when I drove to the Hollywood Vista Motel and left my car on the street. The same beer truck was there but at a different place along the curb. I wondered why it had not been ticketed, or maybe it had and I didn't see it.

"Why didn't you call me?" Dixie asked.

"I didn't know I was supposed to."

She put her arms around me. "I'm afraid."

I held her and patted her. Her whole body seemed to be shaking. "What is it? What's the matter?"

"I do not want to talk about it," she said, flaunting her accent again.

She stood back from me her eyes exploring my face. Then she hugged me again and started to knead my back with her fingers. "But you are here now and everythin' should be all right."

Patty explained that men Merriman's age were never satisfied with the amount and intensity of the sex they got. Men like me have the same kind of problem, especially after I had to turn down someone as sexy as Alice Trugante who was ripping her clothes off for me.

Dixie was shaking and I was holding her tight. Soon I was shaking too, but it was for a different reason. She kissed me and we rolled onto the bed. We started jabbering about everything and nothing. She was telling me about how she was afraid of some kid who was seeing Alice. When I mentioned Normie, she said that he was the one she was talking about. By that time, I had my face buried in her breasts and my hand far under her skirt.

"Sal will protect you," I said.

154

"Nobody can protect me. Only I can protect me – and you can."

"Yeah," I said. We were working our way toward needs that each of us wanted to satisfy, if only for the next half-hour or so. "And who's going to protect me when Sal finds out that we've been in bed together?"

"He will never know," she said. "Never – oh God, that feels good. Nevah. Oh, yes."

She was moving her body and letting me help her off with her panties. She clutched at me, drew me to her, placed me and welcomed me.

She smiled up at me and pushed my hair back from my face. Then her mouth fell open with a deep intake of breath. Her eyes went back. She was satiated, at least partially, and I was nowhere near that point.

"Keep doin' that. Keep lovin' me. Just keep lovin' me," she said.

And I did, not once, but several times. After I smoked a cigarette – just one – I eased off to sleep.

CHAPTER XXVI

"What's going on with Trugante and Cameron?" I asked after one of those times that Dixie woke me during the night.

"What do you mean, 'goin on?'"

"Who's in charge?"

"Why Sal, naturally. Why do you ask?"

"Who's making the deals with Bugsy Siegel?"

"I believe that Sal pays for protection, if that's your meanin'." That was my meaning, and just like that, she told me.

"What's Cameron's stake?"

"You do ask the strangest question in the middle of the night. He runs the call business. It's not the biggest money, but it's the cleanest. Some of those houses down in San Diego..."

"The ones for the sailors?"

"The ones for anybody who happens to have ten dollars." She sat up in bed. Her breasts, so beautifully shaped, were distracting me. "Why are you interested in the business end of all this? Isn't your job to track down that boy who got Alice with child?"

"I suppose it is," I said, but it was also my job to find out who killed Laura. I wanted to know not for the money that Prendergast was paying and the favor I was doing for Sandiri, but I wanted the police to know. I wanted the killers to pay.

"You knew Laura all through the war didn't you?"

"Mister Rick Page, you are askin' far too many questions when we should be doin' other things."

She brought her hand inside my thigh, walked her fingers gently upward, and teased. She brought her lips to mine for a moment. She darted the tip of her sharp tongue against mine. She trailed it over my chin, my neck, my chest.

How you gonna keep 'em down on the farm after they've seen Pareeee? I heard the band in my head, then a drum roll, heading toward a crash of the cymbals.

She had managed to quell my curiosity.

* * * *
When I awoke for the day, she was getting ready to go to Trugante's office, so I took my shower. When I came out, I asked about Laura again.

"I don't like to think about Laura, because I don't like to think about Prendergast, or that ugly little butler of his."

"Why?"

"Because I think he is the one that killed her. He did it for Prendergast."

I wanted to ask if she knew that Albert was Laura's father. Instead I just asked how long she knew Laura.

"Since 1939, dancin' in ball gowns in *Gone with the Wind*. Those were the days."

I knew that Clark Gable epic was not an MGM film, but Louie Mayer might have loaned starlets to Selznick just as he had loaned out Gable.

"And Patty Drake?" I asked her.

"She is older than we are, and she was a real actress, so to speak." She looked at me, almost in anger. Then she went into the bathroom and slammed the door. I dressed while she was in there.

When she came out, she was in bra and girdle and she crossed to the closet to get her dress. She did not speak until she had put on her makeup. Then she turned and looked hard at me.

"One night, Mister Tyree Prendergast paid Michael for all three of us, and I will leave the rest to your imagination."

She pinned her Robin Hood hat to her naturally wavy hair, slipped into her jacket, and started for the door.

"I hope you don't think you will be livin' here with me," she said. I knew why she was angry and it had nothing to do with last night.

"I wasn't planning on living here. And I don't think I'll be calling you unless you call me."

Her body went limp and she put her arms around me. "I'm so sorry. I don't know why I'm actin' this way."

When I left at eight fifteen, she was still there.
* * * *
When I went home. I knew that something was wrong. Someone had looked through my desk and found both my Trugante and Prendergast files. Some of my notes were missing, but there was not much I could do about it except guess who had taken them and wonder why they had.

I called my answering service.

"Some fella named Trugante wants to see you at his house at one o'clock for lunch," the girl said. "He said something about a pregnancy report. What's that mean?"

"It's more than you need to know."

"You don't have to bite my head off."

I called Sandiri and asked him to meet me at the Rexall Drug Store on the corner of Hollywood and Vine.

"I'll buy," I said.

"Too cheap to spring for dinner?"

"I still owe you. What I have won't keep."

"Then I'll be there."

I read the *L.A. Examiner* while I waited. The headline implied that the Black Dahlia's killer was going to surrender, but I didn't believe it. Photos of the postcard allegedly written by the killer were on the front page, along with the photo of another envelope that was addressed to the district attorney.

I was not obsessive about the Black Dahlia case, but I was curious. From time to time, it seemed that the Dahlia was connected with the murders of Laura Fane Prendergast, the taxi driver and Little Georgie. Neither Laura nor Georgie's murders had been reported in the press, but in the back pages, I found an obituary for Laura. They reported that she had died "suddenly." There was no more explanation than that.

It was hard to believe that the police could hide Laura's murder forever, considering who her husband was, but as Sandiri said, I didn't know the city as well as I should, and maybe Prendergast could buy anything. I had already drunk two cups of coffee when he came in and sat across the booth from me.

"What d'ya have that won't keep?"

"You see this?" I showed him the obituary of Laura Prendergast. "When is the world going to know what happened?"

"Never, if I can help it."

After we ordered, I started to roll off a list of what I thought were facts, and he asked me what I thought they meant.

"Cameron works for Trugante," I said. "They are both in the business of prostitution."

"Big surprise."

"I know it's not news to you, but it was news to me last week. I'd barely heard of Cameron, and Trugante was like a ghost, hovering out there someplace. I heard of him and I knew what he did, but I had no idea he was so big."

I started in, step by step. I mentioned how Laura was sold to Prendergast, how she had run away from him and how her father had tried to rescue her. I included how the cab driver, the same one who had his throat slit, had dumped Albert after he picked them up at the Roosevelt. I gave him information that was corroborated either by multiple witnesses or by my own observation. I gave facts first and told him my interpretation of them. Finally I explained what I would do next.

"And you think that's going to solve everything?"

"Not everything, but–"

"All it does is complicate things." He leaned across the table and spoke in low tones. "I have a good idea who did it."

"Then why don't you do something about it?" I said.

"You and me have been working together how long?"

"Over a year this time. A couple of years before the war."

"Right. I told you there are cases that never go to court because of the people involved."

"You said murder never got buried. You said you wanted to work this case because it reached into important bedrooms."

"I didn't lie. I'm still learning like you are. If what you say is right, and I think you might be, there is no way I can soak these people in cyanide."

"Why?"

"They're the wrong people."

"The wrong people? What does that mean?"

"Do you know how much an ordinary cop makes in L.A. County?"

"Not much."

"Right, not much at all."

I thought about my income last year. My clients paid expenses on their cases, but some stiffed me. After I paid for my office, my phone, my answering service and the laundry necessary to do the job, I didn't clear much more than they did. I didn't make as much as a sergeant and I told him that.

"That's a shame. You should take a second job like some of the rest of us."

"You have a second job?"

"Yeah, keeping your ass out of the fire."

"What are you trying to tell me?"

He glanced around the room. Nobody was in the booth behind us. "We were afraid this would happen."

"Afraid what would happen?"

"Me, the lieutenant, some others. We were afraid you'd get into it too far. You have to stop right here. There's too damned much money involved."

"What am I supposed to do, bury it like you do?"

"You know how much money Trugante slithers off to street cops – not to mention a couple of sergeants and a lieutenant? You know how much Prendergast contributed the mayor's campaign? Or how many times Cameron slips a free evening to one, two, or all of the above?"

"You mean to tell me that murder doesn't matter if graft is involved?"

"Some, but not as much as it should. It's according to whose money it is and how much it is. I was hoping we would come up with somebody else."

"You mean there are people you would throw to the wolves?"

"*I* could be thrown to the wolves. And so could you."

I sat back and looked at him. He had always been honest with me, and maybe he was being too honest now. He was telling me to look the other way on three, maybe four murders that had me waking up in the middle of the night with dreams that were playing like movies. Sometimes, the pictures in my head were playing during the day. Even the cab driver whose slit throat I imagined provided matinees with the occasional midnight showings.

I saw the dance of the satyr and the nymph over the dangling body of Laura Prendergast, I remembered the viciousness that had been dished out over the trussed body of Little Georgie, and I thought of Elizabeth Short who had been cut in half.

"I can't just forget about it because there's big money involved."

"Forget about money. Think about your neck. Just give Trugante a report on the potential fathers, but weigh your words carefully."

"I'm planning on it."

"And don't tell him everything."

"Why?"

"Ever heard the expression, 'kill the messenger?'"

"You think he'd do that?"

"He doesn't know you."

"You wouldn't let him kill me – not and let him get away with it. I've known you too long."

"What if I'm not the man you think I am?"

"You are."

"Rick, it's not balls you've go, it's a death wish. You're sticking your head in a noose." He slid from behind the table.

Telling the truth might not be the smart thing to do, but I had seen the bodies. I had seen women lost. I had seen how men made money from them. I might not be able to stop all of it, but maybe I could stop the worst of it. And maybe I could bring peace to the little old man in the bowler hat.

* * * *

A five-story house against a mountain, with a swimming pool on top, and a winding road leading to it was a perfect setting for a twentieth-century fairy tale. I only hoped it would not be a setting for a final *Grand Guignol* performance.

Dixie grinned when I stepped into Mr. Trugante's reception room. "I am *so* sorry about this mornin'."

160

Before I could reply, the door opened, and Trugante stepped from his office.

"It's good to see you, Rick. We'll go up to the solarium. It's a nice day, bright and sunny but not too hot. You can take a dip in the pool after if you like."

In a doubled-breasted pin-stripe suit, Trugante looked more prepared for dinner than for lunch, and I felt underdressed in a sport jacket. He continued speaking while we walked to the elevator. We passed amenities between us, casual on his part, but forced on mine.

Early afternoon was the perfect time for sunbathing, and I expected to see Alice lounging around the pool, but she wasn't there. I was relieved because of what I had to tell her father.

"So, do you have a son-in-law picked out for me?"

He led me to the round table in one corner of the solarium. It was about five yards from the table to the pool. The table was covered with a white tablecloth, set with napkins, silver and empty plates just as in fancy restaurants. There was a low table to his right with a telephone, two manila folders and an intercom box. I think the manila folders were mine.

He gestured for me to sit, and he took a place in the corner with his back to the glass. It was the cowboy Wild Bill Hickok who was always afraid that he would be shot in the back. With Trugante, anyone who wanted to kill him could easily do it with long-range rifle fired from across the Canyon.

"Carlo, wine first," he said

A small man in black slacks and white shirt seemed to step from nowhere behind me and I was startled. He poured the wine for Trugante to taste and Trugante approved. He collected our clean but empty plates and walked away. I saw his reflection in the glass

"*Salute!*" Trugante said in the accent that he rarely showed to such extreme.

"*Salute!*" I said, trying to match the pronunciation.

The wine was dry, perfect.

I knew that the hard part about this was going to be telling him things in an order that would please him early on, and hopefully get him in a good mood for the bad news, and the worse news that would follow.

CHAPTER XXVII

"I've located your future son-in-law."

"I knew you would do that."

"He may not be the man you would prefer, but I think he will be good to your daughter, and she would be good for him, assuming they can get certain appetites under con–"

He knew what he was going to say and he stopped me by putting up his hand. He was angry rather than amused. "I will discuss their habits when I know who he is."

"The boy comes from a decent background. I think he is in love with your daughter in spite of the fact that he is seeing an older woman. I use the word 'older' in its loosest meaning. I learned that she'll be leaving him soon. He'll be upset, but not terribly. He carries pictures of your daughter."

"What kind of pictures?" He said it quickly and as if he suspected there were nude photos of Alice floating through some under-society.

"Not that kind of picture. Pictures when they were together and seemed happy." I started to reach into my jacket, then I asked, "May I?"

"Of course," he said.

I took the photo of Alice and Normie on the beach with Normie holding a surfboard, and I pushed it across the tablecloth.

"When was this taken?" There was something about Trugante's speech, even with its Chicago-Italian accent, that inspired me to speak more clearly, and I was weighing my choice of words.

"A month or two at the most." I gestured over the beach background. "It was too cold for many people to be on the beach. A year ago, the young man was up at Fort Ord in Officer Candidate School. The rumor is that he washed out, but my guess is that the war was over and his father managed to get him discharged instead of having him sent to Japan or Germany for the occupation."

"He's well off, this father?"

"He is in the printing business in Pasadena. He is a regular customer of brothels and call girls."

"Would my people know him?"

"You may have seen him a couple of weeks ago at the Roosevelt Hotel."

Some men might be embarrassed, but not Trugante. He was not the kind of person to be embarrassed about anything he did, although he might be concerned if there was a potential for arrest.

"His name is Norman Merriman, like his father. Sometimes they call him Normie. Sometimes, 'Junior,' but not very often."

"Does my daughter love this boy?"

"She likes him, and that's a start."

"Is he the father of the child?"

"No offense, but short of a blood test, you can't be certain." I almost winced when I let that one out.

"Hmm. A smart boy, but a lazy boy." He was nodding and focusing on the surfboard in the photo. "A boy who sits in the ocean waiting for something to happen will go no further than the beach."

"A good marriage could change all that."

"You say the right words. Would *you* take a blood test?"

"Of course," I said. There was no danger that I was the father.

"He is the one then, huh?"

"As I said–"

"Yes, yes, blood test. Would he make me proud even though he is not Italian?"

"If he's treated right."

Trugante raised his eyebrows at my choice of words. Then, he made a dismissive gesture. "You say he is smart?"

"Yes, sir."

"Then it's settled. I will have someone speak to his parents."

As I wrote both of their addresses on the back of one of my business cards, I explained the situation about Normie and his father.

"Then I will speak to all of them," Trugante said.

Carlo brought our salad, tossed it in a wooden bowl in front of us and put a generous portion on each of our plates. Whatever else Carlo was, he was also a trained waiter. I did not hear his footsteps, but I saw him leave in the reflection from the glass.

I tasted my wine, forked my salad, weighed my words.

"Is there something wrong with the salad, Mister Page?"

"It's very good."

I chewed, thought some more and swallowed. Then I finally spoke, "I've told you the best news."

"And now you will tell me the worst?"

The news I was ready to give was not the worst, and hopefully not the most dangerous to me, but it would lead gently into the worst news.

"Your secretary has betrayed you," I said.

"With you?" He smiled. "It's not a problem. I gave you my permission.

"It's not that kind of betrayal."

"Hmm." He still had salad in his mouth. When he finished chewing, he asked, "Then what kind of betrayal?"

"Someone has put her as a spy in your midst." Those were the words I used. They sounded as if they came from a movie or a radio program and I was embarrassed.

"Spy?" He raised his eyebrows, pretending to be blasé, but he was far from it. He breathed more deeply and his cheeks went to a tinge of pink. His fingers began to shake almost imperceptibly.

"A spy for who? For the police? The Hungarians? The Greeks? Siegel and the Las Vegans?"

I heard the elevator door open and I turned to see Michael Cameron coming toward us. I wanted to get out the whole story, but there was not enough time.

"Mister Trugante," Cameron said. "Ah, and *Mis*ter Page!"

"Sit and have some wine with us," Trugante said.

Cameron offered his clammy hand.

There were no extra place settings, but there were extra glasses, and Trugante poured for him.

"Very good," Cameron said after he tasted it.

"Mister Page says that Miss Joy has betrayed us," Trugante said.

"Betrayed?"

"Who with, Mister Page? Who is she working for?" Trugante asked.

I was stuck, but I thought it was best to tell him. "With Mister Cameron," I said.

For the next few seconds, the only sound in the solarium was the bubbling of the pools filtration system.

"He's trying to take over all of your enterprises," I said.

"We should have killed this bastard when we had a chance," Cameron said. His facial expression twisted to a vicious anger.

"Let him speak."

"When he tells lies?"

"I said let him speak. Then I will determine what to do with him."

"Mister Cameron's holding back on the new recruits for your houses. He's taking the best of them and training them in West Hollywood. He moved Miss Joy out of her own house and–"

"She moved to a motel," Trugante said, and he shrugged.

"He took the house so they could open a new brothel. He wants your entire business for himself."

Trugante seemed amused, and Cameron relaxed.

"He sells them into a kind of slavery. He sold a girl to Tyree Prendergast, but she refused to stay with him even though she married him. Others buy them to amuse themselves. Miss Joy tracks new ones and solicits them. He keeps the best for–"

"You said that," Trugante said.

I was sitting between him and Cameron. Both seemed relaxed, while I talked on and on like a guilty man desperate to save his life.

"And why would she do that?" Cameron asked.

I explained that Cameron owned the Wilshire Taxi Company, and that Paul France, the murdered driver, was virtually Cameron's private chauffeur. "I'm sure that Dixie had access to that cab, because she was the one who cut his throat."

Cameron chuckled, and Trugante gestured for silence.

While I waited, thoughts went through my head that I didn't say aloud. The first night I saw her at her house on Doheny, she was coming from Sunset in a Yellow Cab – not a Wilshire cab as would be her usual. It took a while, but I finally figured that she had murdered Paul France on the lot behind my office across the street from the KNX radio studios. It was how KNX got the news so quickly.

When she heard it, I saw her grin. I had no idea how she and Cameron knew that he had given me the correct address, just as I had no idea how I had transposed the house numbers.

They knew that I was looking for Laura, which was why they had killed France on my lot. It was my first warning, but I didn't get it, which was why they followed me to Santa Monica and tossed me off the pier. They knew who I was, but they didn't know anything about me. That was Cameron and Dixie's mistake. Now I seemed to be making mistakes of my own.

"She did this for you, Michael?" Trugante said, grinning.

"Of course she did," Cameron said and he chuckled. He was playing it perfectly and I was talking myself deeper into trouble.

In the reflection from the glass, I was aware that Carlo of the soft steps was standing directly behind me. He might have a blackjack, a gun, a garrote or all three. To jump up and fight was useless. I had no gun and no way to get through Trugante's small army to my car.

"He seduced your daughter before the war and he's been with her many times since." It was true, but I was trying to put myself in a better position by putting Cameron in a worse one. It didn't seem to be working.

"Alice was only fourteen before the war," Cameron said.

"And she's still in love with you."

"I haven't seen her in–"

"In what? Weeks? Days? You still see her. You like the fact that you're taking advantage of Salvatore Trugante's daughter, don't you."

Trugante looked hard across the table at me. "I think you've talked long enough, Mister Page... What do you think of all this?" He had turned to Cameron and he waved his arm as if the facts were scattered around the solarium and over the pool.

"A guy begging for his life," Cameron said.

"Yes," Trugante said.

Carlo was still behind me, ready to do whatever it was he had to do, but I was ready for his move if he made one.

"I think you've talked long enough, Mister Page," Trugante said.

"But—"

"A guy begging for his life," Cameron said again, and he laughed.

"Very good, Michael. But who should be the beggar?"

Cameron knew Trugante better than I did, and he assessed his situation. Then in a motion so quick that I barely saw it, he kicked back the chair, reached under his jacket, and pulled out an automatic pistol. I thought he was going to shoot me, but he fired at Carlo. Carlo banged back against the wall, then fell face-down on the tiles.

I didn't think Cameron had a chance to get away, not with four flights of stairs, a half-dozen bodyguards and a winding road between him and freedom. But he had Dixie downstairs, and I didn't know what she might do to help him. She and Cameron had killed Laura and Little Georgie, and I was sure that they had killed others just for the pleasure of it.

He started to back toward the elevator.

Trugante rose from his chair and Cameron swung the weapon toward him.

I was unwilling to put my fate in Cameron's hands and in a move that was as stupid as it was quick, I charged at him. He fired and missed, and I tackled him, banging him against a planter of roses and tumbling us both into thorns that scratched my face and hands. We struggled for the gun, but it fell free and clacked to the tiles.

I grabbed him, spun him around, and smashed his face against the glass of the solarium. The glass didn't break, but a trail of blood smeared down the pane. I let him go and I stepped back.

When he turned toward me, he had a knife and he threw it at me. When I ducked, he dove for the automatic that Trugante was already reaching for. Cameron got there first, rolled, and came to his feet. I was standing too. He pointed the gun at Trugante, but I was not going to give him a chance to use it. I charged again, this time banging just his arm against the concrete planter. The gun fired and hit the glass, which must be bulletproof because the shell ricocheted and struck something at the other end of the solarium. I banged his wrist hard against the planter again, and the gun bounced free.

I pulled him around the planter and toward the pool, but he pulled me in with him. With his arm around my neck, he held me under water. I grabbed his testicles. He let me loose, and I came to the surface. Trugante held the automatic now, but he just stood there watching us, not aiming the gun, not helping me but not helping Cameron either.

I twisted out of Cameron's grasp. I was behind him and I was holding him under. The blood from his face discolored the water.

"Enough!" Trugante shouted. "He'll be taken care of. Don't let him drown. Drag him out of there."

I held him long enough to know that he could not come back at me. I was out of breath, and so was he, but he was groggy. I dragged him to the shallow end and pushed him onto the tiles. Finally, I pulled myself up and sat on the edge of the pool.

"What you tell me, is it true?" Trugante asked.

"Yes," I said, after I could breath.

"Carlo, are you all right?"

Carlo grunted. He was trying to stand and he was holding his bloody side where Cameron had shot him. I struggled to my feet. Trugante went to the intercom and told someone to come up. I kept an eye on Cameron who lay sprawled like a beached dolphin.

"All of this was in the notes that Carlo took from your files. Why did you not tell me the truth earlier? I might have made Michael marry her."

"And how long would he live after the wedding?" I was still lying on my side and trying to catch my breath.

"Yes, how long? He is quite a charmer."

"Always the charmer," I said.

One of Trugante's other soldiers stepped from the elevator, his gun drawn. He looked confused.

"Get the doctor for these men," he commanded.

"Of course." The guy bowed his head to Trugante and returned to the elevator.

"I have long suspected this business with Alice and Michael, but I did not know about when she was a young girl... You are finished here, Mister Page, but one more thing – that fellow in the bowler hat – are you certain he did not kill this Laura?"

"He was her father."

"Yes, your notes. It must have been difficult for him."

"It was difficult for all of us."

"But for a father most of all," Trugante said. "I would like you to take a shower, get some fresh clothes. When you are ready we will send you home."

Send me home? It sounded as if I had been a bad boy, but maybe I had.

* * * *

Trugante directed me to a changing room with a shower, where I slipped into some clothes that were not my style, but they fit.

When I went through his office a half-hour later, Dixie was not there.

On Hollywood Boulevard and all the way back to my apartment, another car followed me. Before I got out, I drew the automatic from under the seat. I was ready for anything, but it was Sandiri who stepped from behind the wheel.

"You lived through it," he said. He looked at the peg-legged pants and the flowered shirt. "Nice outfit."

"I'm going to the beach later, maybe a dance tonight. What were you going to do? Climb the mountain if you heard gunshots?"

"From outside that place, you don't hear gunshots. But they wouldn't have shot you. It would have been the garrote."

"Thanks for the thought."

"How'd you make out with Uncle Sal?"

"He's an all right guy. Well, kind of all right. Who calls him Uncle Sal?"

"His nephews."

"You're kidding? What took you so long to tell me that?"

"I didn't want you going to hell thinking a relative of mine did you in. What did you tell him?"

"Everything. He's a good listener. And Cameron..."

"What about Cameron?"

"Nothing," I said.

* * * *

The next morning, I picked up the *Examiner*. The Dahlia was still in the headline, because the killer hadn't shown up as he promised, but there was another front-page story. "Hollywood Playboy and girl friend dead in auto crash," the caption read.

I glanced at the article.

"The bodies of Michael Cameron, Hollywood playboy, and his girl friend, former starlet Dixie Joy, were found early this morning. Their automobile crashed into a wall off of Sepulveda Boulevard. Police think that..."

It was not necessary for me to read the rest of the article, but I needed the details, even if I knew them to be false. I thought about what Sandiri had told me many times. The LAPD didn't always match the right criminal with the right crime, but every crook eventually paid a price.

At Laura's intimate funeral, Tyree Prendergast and Albert Fane were the only men who shed tears. I misted a little, but I managed to hold

back.   After Laura was safely interred at a San Fernando Valley
Cemetery, I showed them the newspaper without comment.

"I saw that, Mister Page. You've well earned your advance, both
advances," Tyree Prendergast said.

"It was just a matter of fate carrying out justice."

"Thank you," Albert said softly. He held the door and Prendergast
climbed into the limousine.

On my way back to the car, Sandiri joined me for the walk. He was
carrying a copy of a different paper, with the same stories on the front
page.

"I take it you saw this?" he said.

"Poetic justice," I said.

"That uncle of mine is one hell of a poet."

We stood at his car. "What happened with that Dahlia guy that was
supposed to be turning himself in?" I asked.

"Never showed up. The whole letter thing was a hoax. There's a lot
of murders in L.A. that'll never be solved."

"And a lot that nobody's even going to know about," I said. "Did you
get an invitation to Alice Trugante's wedding?"

"Yeah, and Uncle Sal wants me to go to work for him, but I don't
think so. I suggested you might like to take Cameron's place."

"No thanks," I said.

"You might find that whore with a heart of gold that you're always
looking for."

"I'll look someplace else."

Cameron was out of the picture and so was Dixie Joy. But there were
others who never paid, and justice would have to wait for them.
Trugante was still in business too, and I wondered if in a sense, he was
any less guilty than they were.

Millions of people already knew about the death of Elizabeth Short,
but who would ever know of Laura Fane or Little Georgie whose
murders had been committed in the shadow of the Black Dahlia? For
that matter, did that or even the Dahlia herself make a difference in the
grand scheme of the universe?

Maybe not – but I had to keep working as if they did.

CPSIA information can be obtained
at www.ICGtesting.com
Printed in the USA
FSOW01n0936040217
30401FS